THE DAY
OF THE
MONARCH

THE DAY OF THE MONARCH

Robert E. Hill

iUniverse, Inc.
Bloomington

THE DAY OF THE MONARCH

iUniverse books may be ordered through booksellers or by contacting:

iUniverse
1663 Liberty Drive
Bloomington, IN 47403
www.iuniverse.com
1-800-Authors (1-800-288-4677)

ISBN: 978-1-4759-7476-8 (sc)
ISBN: 978-1-4759-7478-2 (hc)
ISBN: 978-1-4759-7477-5 (ebk)

Library of Congress Control Number: 2013902855

Printed in the United States of America

iUniverse rev. date: 02/19/2013

DEDICATED TO:

Abigail Records, my wonderful granddaughter, every time I think of you I smile.

To Angela Records my amazing daughter, every time I think of you I'm amazed and proud.

To Harlan Hill, my son and best friend, every time I think of you I think I can accomplish anything.

To Eric Hill (1980-2000), my son and my heart, every time I think of you I think of Heaven and how I can't wait to join you there.

Acknowledgments

Cover Design—Ashley Hesch\Robert Hill

Content Contributor—Shane Lattin

Warren Ranch Image—Chapter 7—Courtesy George Warren

Sugar Bars Image—Chapter 8—Courtesy George Warren

Network Puzzle Image—Chapter 16—Courtesy of Renjith Krishnan\FreeDigitalPhotos.net

Mars Rover Image—Chapter 19—Courtesy NASA

International Space Station Image—Chapter 28—Courtesy NASA

Mars Image—Chapter 29—Courtesy NASA

CHAPTER ONE

THE LAST CHRISTMAS

Perry, Oklahoma, to some, is a wide spot on Interstate 35 in North Eastern Oklahoma. It is home to just over 5,000 of the finest people on the planet. Its claim to fame is that it's the smallest town in Oklahoma with a daily newspaper and it was Perry's very own law enforcement that arrested Timothy McVeigh after he blew up the Federal Building in Oklahoma City. It is also home to the Charles Machine Works, the headquarters and manufacturing center for the world-renowned Ditch Witch trenchers.

The people here seem to run at a different speed than those in the bigger cities and that's something that they are very proud of.

This particular Christmas season was unusually cold and had an overabundance of snow and rain. Snowplows and tire chains were as common as Christmas trees and candy canes.

For my family it was Christmas, and the snow and the cold made it even more exciting and helped to draw the family even closer together.

We are the Tate family and we are just a typical American family. We are kind of like the ones that you imagine when you think of a family sitting in front of a fireplace drinking hot chocolate and playing board games. We live on a farm on the south side of Perry and with 240 acres it is a full time job for the family to keep it going.

Jerry Tate is my dad. He's a farmer. Making things grow is what he does best and he has spent his whole life on this farm doing just that. His great Grandfather built this farm and it has been passed down from son to son and now it was dad's turn.

Angela is my mother. She's also interested in making things grow. She has worked hard all her life and now has a PhD in Horticulture from Texas A & M University. The farm is the perfect place to put her theories to the test.

Erica is my older sister. At 16 she is at that point where she knows more than she will ever know again. Boys are her main topic of study and she is trying to learn all she can.

I'm Abby and daughter number two. At 12 years old I am considered by most to be normal but my dad says I'm way too smart for my age. I spend my spare time taking things apart to see how they work. I am fascinated by things outside of our universe and yet I think I'm very down to earth. I love playing soccer, softball, and racing go-carts. With two dogs, Flash, a Dachshund, and Howie, a Golden Retriever, I'm the animal lover of the family.

Harlan is my brother and the youngest. At six years old, Harlan has already figured out how to manipulate his two sisters and of course, being the youngest, he always seems to get breaks that his sisters never get. Like, recently my mom put her foot down and said no more dogs. Of course Harlan decided he wanted a dog and mom decided to bend her rule and Harlan got a dog too. His name is Maynard. He's an English bulldog that pretty well goes wherever he wants and does whatever he wants.

Christmas has always been my favorite time of year. Although mom and dad has instilled in our minds what the real meaning of Christmas is and how important it is, when you're a kid, getting that present you so desperately have to have is far more a greater miracle than the Son of God coming to earth to hang out with His people. But at Christmas there is always real magic in the air. The greatest food, the smell of a pine tree in the living room, people laughing and being nice to each other, family from far and wide calling or coming by to wish you well, waiting for mom and dad to leave the room so I can shake my presents and try to figure out what they are, and the most magical of them all, two weeks off from school.

This Christmas Eve was no different than any other, until the power went out. I was right in the middle of watching my favorite show, Victorious, when everything went dark. After about fifteen minutes of setting in the dark I decided to check things out, so I walked outside like I had done so many times before. As I walked into the blackness that surrounded our country home I was amazed at how the cold and darkness felt like it could have been cut with a knife. It was so crisp. No gray. Just black and white. A mixture of silence, snow, and little dots of light. The stars were so bright and the sky was so dark. The grass was frozen and it made loud crunches as I walked around.

The normal sounds that would flow around the farm and entertain me with the game of trying to guess what they were weren't there. No planes flashing across the sky, no coyotes howling in the distance. Just a silent satellite streaking across the sky. How can a world so big be so quiet?

Harlan walked out the back door and when he was unable to see me he started to panic.

"Boo Boo, Boo Boo, where are you?" he started to scream.

"I'm right here," I said and walked over to him.

Boo-Boo is his nickname for me and soon it caught on and mom, dad, and Erica forgot my real name and just called me Boo-Boo.

"Why is it so dark out here?" He asks.

"Well, the power is out everywhere so there is no yard light, no lights on the pump house, and I guess there is no light at the airport so there are no planes in the sky." I said.

"Why is it so quiet?" He asks.

"I'm not sure. I think all the animals have already gone to bed so they can get up early in the morning to see what presents they got."

"Boo-Boo, if the earth is spinning around like they say it is, then why doesn't it make a noise when it turns? Shouldn't the trees moving through the air have to make a sound? And if it is truly spinning then when I jump up why don't I land in a different spot when I come down? Because the earth turned while I was in the air." He says.

"Where do you come up with these questions? You sure you're only six?"

"Mom says I'm just like you." He says.

"Well you are really cute."

"I think she meant really smart." He says.

"OK big guy it's time to go in."

Harlan and I walked back into the house. Everything is very dark but I see a candle light flickering and moving around as dad walks by.

"So what's going on Dad?" I said. "Why is there no power?"

"I don't know yet," Dad said. "It may be out for a while, so I'm going down to the basement to start the generator. Your mom and Erica are in the kitchen. There is enough heat coming from the kitchen stove to keep everybody warm until I can get the generator started."

"Wasn't that supposed to start up automatically when the power went off?" I said. "It seems technology works best when you don't need it."

"I'm sure the power company will have the power back up shortly," Dad said. "Probably ice taking down a power line somewhere and it glitched the system."

As Dad walks down the stairs to the basement, I walk to the kitchen to join the rest of the family. The kitchen is actually kind of neat, yet spooky, with all the candles sitting around.

"Mom, you're taking this Christmas thing to far," I said. "Just because there was no electricity at the first Christmas doesn't mean we need to <u>live</u> the experience now!"

Mom is standing by the stove with the oven door open.

"Come over here and get warm," Mom says.

"Why does the stove work and nothing else does?" Harlan asks.

"The stove runs on butane and not electricity," Erica says.

"We are country folk, we don't have one of them newfangled electric stoves that you read about in the Sears Catalog," I said.

"If we had one of them we would be very cold right now," mom says.

A faint rumbling sound comes up from the basement and the lights flicker on. Dad comes up the basement stairs and starts spewing out commands.

"Turn off everything electrical. The only thing that needs to be on is a few lights and the heating system. There should be enough fuel in the generator to last about four hours, but I'm sure the power company will have the power restored long before then," Dad said.

"Can we turn the Christmas tree lights back on?" Harlan asks.

"I guess we can. It is Christmas Eve. But we are turning in early tonight. Even if the power comes back on we are still going to bed early," Dad says.

"I know you three and you're going to get up before dawn to see what you have under the tree," Mom says.

"With no electricity I will be bored to sleep in an hour," Erica says.

Mom goes over to the closet and sorts through boxes until she finds the one she wants.

"Ok guys, who's up for a game of Risk?" Mom asks.

We all three start mumbling, but we all get up and walk to the kitchen table and set down ready to play. After about two hours of Risk, dad decided we should head for bed.

After about ten minutes of freezing in our own beds, everyone moved into mom and dad's room so we could conserve heat. We all piled into their bed to share our body heat and Maynard, Flash, and Howie, decided to get into the act so they joined us. Sometime during the night Flash and Howie got irritated with all the squirming and bailed off the bed. Maynard decided to stick it out. He had staked claim to his area and he wasn't going to give it up.

Christmas morning was so cold and being warm under the covers was far better than walking barefoot on an ice-cold floor, but Harlan, realizing it was Christmas morning, began digging out from the bottom of the pile. Nothing was going to get in his way. Santa Claus didn't need electricity to make his rounds and he was sure the tree would be standing in the middle of a treasure trove of presents. So we all headed to the living room and no one even stopped to consider how the presents got under the tree when mom and dad never left the bed all night.

Christmas day was finally here. The sun was up so we had light coming through the windows and the siege at the bottom of the Christmas tree had begun.

As usual everyone got what he or she had asked for. And as usual mom and dad had spent way too much money on us. We already had more than we needed and like most kids our age we just kept asking for more.

Mom got busy cooking her fabulous Christmas dinner. We always called it dinner for some reason but we always ate it at like 1:00 pm. No one was going to wait until dinner to eat this.

My mom's the best cook on the planet and when it came to Christmas she spared nothing. We always have turkey and ham at the same meal. Then you throw in the dressing, cranberries, green beans, rolls, potatoes, pumpkin pie, pecan pie, and candied yams. You'd think we were having the whole town over for Christmas. But no one complained and it was always gone before the New Year started.

After the great meal things got real quiet. There was no football game on TV because there was no TV. Everyone was in kind of a food-induced coma.

Dad decided we needed to find out when this was all going to be over so he tried to get one of the radios working but none would. He dug out an old antique radio that granny had left him and tried it. We all got really excited when we started hearing amplified static coming out of the speaker. There were no broadcasts. Nothing. Finally down at the low end of the dial we here a faint beeping. Dad tuned it in the best he could and for about an hour we set and listened to the beeping. Finally a voice came on and said that this was the Emergency Broadcast System stay tuned for a message. About an hour later the voice came on again and said the same thing. *How weird is this?* I thought. *Where was everyone? What had happened?*

"Dad can we go somewhere and see what's going on? Obviously this is not a normal power outage and we can't just sit here." I said.

Dad said that he agreed but thought it best we stay here at home.

"I'll leave in a moment and drive down to the gas station and if there is no one there I'll drive over to the Hargrave's farm and see what they know." Dad says.

Around three that afternoon the neighbor's pickup, an ugly yellow 71 Ford, pulls into our driveway. Joslyn Bevil and her son Shane got out of the truck and made their way to the front door. Joslyn is my mother's best friend and Shane is my best guy friend. Even though their farm was a mile down the road we had grown up together. He was a computer nerd extraordinaire and he had even won a computer hacking contest when he was ten.

It was not uncommon for him to ride along with his mother when she came to visit, but this time I was sensing something was wrong. He had a very weird look on his face. The only time

I had seen this look was when he had electrocuted his dad's prize pig.

As soon as they got in the house he wanted to go upstairs to my room. He grabbed me by the hand and practically dragged me up the stairs.

"What's up dude? Chill a little!" I said.

"Abby I think I messed up really bad." Shane said.

"What in the world did you do now?" I ask.

"You know that punk David Bennett that's always trying to punk me out?" Shane said.

"Yes." I said.

"You know that Bennett, Jeff, and Gordon stole my dog Zea right?" Shane said.

"I know you think they did." I said.

"They posted a picture of Zea online." Shane said.

"So what'd you do?" I said.

"I think I messed up bad." Shane said.

"What'd you do Shane? You didn't kill them. Please God tell me you didn't kill them." I said.

"No, I didn't kill them. I had this really wild computer virus that I was playing around with for the next hacker's convention. Really nasty. The kind of nasty the government would love to get a hold of. Not only does it erase the data that's on your computer, but as it leaves it generates an EMF pulse that wipes out all the millions of junctions that make up the millions of discrete devices that make up your computer." Shane said.

"English please," I said.

"It destroys your microprocessor and ram chips." Shane said.

"So you sent this virus to these three dudes and it broke their computers. Big deal. How will they ever prove it was you?" I said.

"First off, why do you think they care if they can prove it was me? They will kill me without proof. Second, the virus caused this whole power outage that we're in the middle of." Shane said.

An awkward 10 seconds of silence follows Shane's last statement then I burst out laughing, rolling on my bed.

"You think you caused the power blackout with your little virus?" I ask.

"It's true. Within 10 minutes after pushing the virus, my computer died. Then the T.V., and then the power." Shane said.

"Come on Shane, you don't really think you caused this power outage?" I said.

"I'm sure of it." Shane said.

"Come on! This thing is affecting people all over this area, maybe the state." I said.

"The State. Haven't you been listening to the Emergence broadcasting station on your radio? This thing has spread all over the world." Shane said.

I am still laughing, as I try to ask a question.

"So you are saying your virus," Shane interrupts and says, "The Monarch Butterfly Virus."

"I'm sorry what" I ask. "Butterfly. You think you just broke the whole world and you call it <u>The Butterfly Virus.</u> I need to start writing this stuff down this would make a good book. <u>Cracked out story of the week.</u>" I said.

"It's not funny," Shane says. "I call it the Monarch Virus after the Monarch Butterfly because Mr. McGee is always talking about the butterfly effect in class. You know, if a butterfly flaps its wings will it cause a hurricane somewhere in the future?"

"Ha Ha Ha. This just gets gooder and gooder. Did you drink wine with Christmas dinner or did you get into your mom's <u>happy</u> pills again?" I said.

"I'm Serious. Ok don't believe me. Let me show you proof." Shane says.

"Ok world destroyer show me some proof."

"All right, have you turned on your computer since the power outage?" Shane asks.

"Yes."

"Did it come up?" Shane asks.

"No there's a power outage, remember."

"Yes, but your dad has a generator running right?" Shane asks.

"True."

"How about your laptop. Have you turned it on since the power outage?" Shane asks.

"Yes."

"Did it come up?" Shane asks.

"No."

"It runs off battery if there is no power right?" Shane asks.

"True."

"Why didn't it come up?" Shane asks.

"I don't know maybe the battery was dead."

"Even if the Internet is down and the power is down it should still come up and run until the battery goes down right?" Shane asks.

"Sure."

"It doesn't because it has been wiped out because it was connected to the Internet when it started. So if we can find a computer that hasn't been turned on since the power outage then it should be okay right." Shane asks.

"You say so,"

"Do you have a computer that hasn't been turned on lately?" Shane asks.

"Erica's laptop probably hasn't been turned on since she got it. Mom and dad gave it to her to take to school and use for studying. She never studies." I said.

"Where is it?" Shane asks.

They get up and go into Erica's room. Erica is sitting in front of her mirror working on her eyebrows.

"I need your laptop." I said.

"What?" Erica asks.

"I need to see your laptop!" I said harshly.

"Okay rude, it's under the bed." Erica said.

I look under the bed and drag out the laptop. I open it up and Shane grabs my hand.

"Don't turn it on yet. Turn off the Wi-Fi card first. If you turn it on with the Wi-Fi card enabled it will connect to the Internet and be destroyed." Shane said.

I searched the edges of the computer until I find the Wi-Fi switch. I turn it off and then look at Shane.

"Now?"

"Yes go ahead." Shane said.

I turn the laptop on. It does its normal whirling and twitching and then the background image of BTR pops up.

"See its working fine. Battery is about half drained but it seems to work fine." I said.

Shane looks at me and says, "Turn on the Wi-Fi card."

I slide my hand down and turn on the Wi-Fi card. Nothing happens. I start singing "Paranoia is in bloom the transmissions will resume".

Then I break out laughing. Then the screen goes black, hard drive light flashes brightly, and then it's dead.

"Oh crap." I said.

Perry Daily Journal

Children's clothes needed

'Clothing for a Cause' will receive donations Saturday

CHAPTER TWO

NO NEWS WAS GOOD NEWS

From outside the window comes the sound of three short burst from a siren. Erica gets up and her and Shane walk over to the window to see what's going on. As they look down at the front yard they see the sheriff getting out of his car and walking toward my dad. My dad is standing next to a large fuel tank putting fuel into 5-gallon gas cans. He takes off his gloves and sticks out his hand to the approaching Sheriff.

Erica, Shane, and I, come running out the front door to where her dad, Harlan and the sheriff are standing.

"What's going on?" Erica asks.

"Everything's cool. The sheriff has just stopped by to tell us about a meeting in Town Square tomorrow. He wants everyone to be there and since communications are down, he is going house-to-house telling people to be there." Dad says.

"So what's the meeting about?" I ask.

"It's about the loss of power and what's being done about it." The sheriff says.

"So why is there no power?" I ask.

"We're not sure. Some are saying it was just some sort of chain reaction started by one of the power stations but I don't think so." The sheriff says.

"What do you think is going on?" Shane asked.

"I don't know for sure but I know that a power plant going off line might cause a chain reaction that trips other power plants and you know, a domino effect takes place, but this isn't like that." The sheriff says.

"Why not?" I ask.

"Power plants going off line don't cause electronic systems to fail. I mean, how could that be?" The sheriff says.

"They fail because there is no power." Erica says.

"Then why don't they start working when you restore the power? Have you tried your computers, TV, iPad, anything like that since you fired up the generators?" The sheriff asks.

"There all dead," I said.

"Right! I plugged in the old antique radio that my mother left me and it works. Only thing I can get is those emergence broadcast messages but it works," Dad says.

"Does the radio in your old truck still work?" The sheriff asks.

"Yea, it's the same, only the emergence messages." Dad says.

"How about your wife's new Lexus?" The sheriff asks.

"No, not only is the radio deader than a hammer her car want even start." Dad says.

"Your truck is from the 60's and it has an analog radio in it. It's just like your mothers old radio, analog. However Angie's Lexus has one of those all digital satellite radios in it." The sheriff says.

"So what are you saying Sheriff?" I ask.

"I'm just saying it's weird that all this old technology is still functioning and all this newfangled Internet connected digital stuff is fried. There is no way a power plant getting overloaded can cause such a thing." The sheriff says.

"So what do you think caused all this?" I ask.

"I think it's some sort of Cyber Terrorist attack." The sheriff says.

"Terrorist attack?" I ask?

"Yea, you know, al-Qaeda or one of those groups over there that wants to do us harm." The sheriff says.

Shane is acting very nervous and ask, "Shouldn't they be able to find out who did something like that? I'm sure they left some kind of trail and they will find out who did it sooner or later."

"Finding them is not the problem right now, surviving this is the big problem." The sheriff says.

"Why" Erica asked. "Can't they just re-boot and be back in business?"

"I hope so." The sheriff says.

"I'm sure the government has protections in place for this kind of thing." Shane says.

"I'm sure they do son," The sheriff says.

"Dad, why does my iPad still work? I mean it's not old and isn't it digital?" Harlan asks.

Shane jumps in with; "It hasn't been connected to the Internet."

The sheriff gives Shane a quizzical look and asks, "What do you mean?"

"I'm just saying it seems that it's not just digital things that have been destroyed. It seems to be things which were or are connected to the internet or a network in some way and of course the only thing you connect to the internet is digital." Shane says.

"So you're Shane, right?" The sheriff asks.

"Yes sir." Shane replies.

"I've heard about you. I hear you are very smart on this computer stuff." The sheriff says.

"Not really." Shane replies.

"He's a genius on computers." I said.

"So what do you make of all this? Do you think it's all due to a power failure?" The sheriff asks Shane.

"No. I think the power failure is a result of it." Shane replies.

"It?" The sheriff asks.

"I just think something else caused the power grid to go down. People don't seem to realize the role computers play in their everyday life." Shane says.

"What do you mean?" The sheriff asks.

"In a power plant you have huge generators that generate power for all of us to use. Those generators are very complicated devices. They have to turn at a certain speed so it has to be monitored at all times. That used to be done by a guy watching a dial on his control panel, now a computer does it automatically. They bring up generators as the need for power goes up and they turn off generators when there is less of a need. This used to be done by a guy watching a load gage on a panel. Now a computer does it automatically. These generators have to be brought up and down and synched together properly. If that doesn't happen you can get a surge of power that will wipe out stuff downstream to it. So, our power plant is connected to other power plants to better balance the load and usage across the country. How are these power plants connected?"

"By computer." Harlan answers.

"Correct." Shane replies. "These computers are connected to each other by a network. Now in most cases a private fiber cable that's owned and controlled by the power company connects them together but they are all connected together nonetheless.

Now, there is a need for remote access to these computers for monitoring and even maintenance. So the power companies use software like RDP to connect to them. How does this happen when the technician is in Colorado and the power plant is in Perry. The Internet. More recently they are putting everything in the cloud."

"So what are you saying?" Dad asks.

"If someone released a smart enough virus on the Internet that kills computers, that virus could go right down the Internet into the private fiber of the Power Company and start picking off their computers. The power plant either automatically shuts down to protect itself or if the computer fails in such a way it could turn on the wrong thing at the wrong time and overload the system. All of this could happen in seconds and the cleanup could take years. The same scenario applies to the Natural Gas companies and the water companies."

"How old are you?" The sheriff asks.

"Twelve." Shane replies.

"How did you get so freaking smart?" The sheriff asks. "Actually I did a report on this last semester in school." Shane says.

"So do you think that's what happened?" The sheriff asks.

"Yes." Shane replies.

"Wow! You sound sure." The sheriff replies.

"You can use this same scenario with the television companies and cell phones facilities, communications. If you watch a movie on H.B.O. It is being played off of a hard drive in some data center somewhere. If you dial your cell phone it digitizes the numbers you push and transmits them to a cell tower where they are received and translated by an interface that is running on some type of computer or microprocessor that sends it over a network to a telephone switch that is made up of computers that are connected to other computers. They are all connected to the Internet somehow or some way and in a sense they are all connected together. So if that happened you would see exactly what we are seeing right now."

"Wow, I've talked to everybody from the governor on down and the only person that has made any sense is a twelve-year-old kid. Kid we will all be working for you one of these days," the sheriff says while chuckling. "I have to move on, but if you folks need anything just let me know."

"Ok we will sheriff thanks for stopping by." Dad says.

"Let's go back in where it's warm. I'll see if mom can whip up some hot chocolate, then we can discuss this some more. You know, before they come to take you away." I said.

"They don't know it was me and without their computers they can't figure out who did it." Shane says.

We get our hot chocolate and head into my room. Harlan try's to follow but I tell him to get lost.

"Ok let's say that I believe you. I mean, I think you are smart enough to do it, but I'm having a hard time believing that you just killed the Internet and disabled the whole world. You know it's something that I don't have to deal with every day." I said.

"We'll all I can tell you is that when I hit the return key to send the Monarch to those jerks everything started dying." Shane says.

"So you couldn't have just erased their hard drives, or signed them up for a ten-year subscription to Ballet Monthly, you had to kill their computers?"

"They have Zea Abby, and they deserved it." Shane says.

"I understand, but as smart as you are, I mean you're smart enough to write the stupid virus but not smart enough to know that it was going to cause a major world malfunction." I said.

"So how are you going to fix it?" I ask.

"The problem is that the virus determines where it's at and what it is that contains it. So if it senses it's on a computer it destroys it. If it senses that it is on a router or switching device then it cloaks itself and just sets there waiting on a new victim. No one can detect it on the router so they will think it's clean and hook up a new computer and zap. Now some of these routers and switches are setting on satellites out in space, which makes it very difficult to replace. Also, if you miss one, then turn on a new router that somehow gets connected to that router then all the new stuff gets infected and you're back to square one."

"So, how are you going to fix it?" I reiterate.

"I can't." Shane says. "I mean, even if I could set down at a computer and come up with some kind of antivirus, there is no way to deploy it because there is no power, which means all those routers and switches are off."

"Except for those in orbit." I said. "Please don't tell me those are all shut down to?" I said.

"No they have their own power up there."

"What about the people in the International Space Station, have you destroyed their computers to?"

"Possible." Shane replies.

"Do you know what they are going to do to you if they find out you caused this? I bet they will sit around and come up with new and special ways to punish you for this."

Shane's mom walks into the room.

"We have to take off Shane." Joslyn says.

"Ok."

"Are you ok? You look like you're sick or something?" Joslyn asks Shane.

"I'm fine." Shane says.

"You're all pale looking. Here let me touch your forehead and see if you have a fever."

Shane gets up and pushes his mother's arm back. He has tears in his eyes and he takes off running out of the room.

"What's going on?" Joslyn asks me.

"I don't know he seems to be weirded out about something. You know Shane he doesn't open up much." I said.

"Ok I'll find out. We will see you later." Joslyn says.

CHAPTER THREE

PERRY TOWN SQUARE

The Perry Town Square is one of my favorite places on the planet. It is so quiet and peaceful with beautiful trees, park benches, green grass, an official hopscotch area, and old buildings like the County Courthouse.

I always love coming to the square. In the past it usually represented a fun time like a carnival, square dancing, a barbecue, or even a rock band performing. Dad always tells us about the time he came here with his dad to see Buster Keaton.

Buster Keaton is another one of Perry's claims to fame. He was a very popular actor\director in the 1920's. Now days I guess he is considered to be one of the top seven directors of all time, and he was from Perry, of course. I only knew of him from dad's recollections of him but dad said the guy never smiled. Not just in his movies but in real life. How weird is that? How can you go through life and not find something to smile about? Although, there were very few smiles here today.

As we arrive people are milling around talking to each other. The park, in the center of the square, has a small amphitheater that would seat about a hundred people. It has a stage that could hold the choir from the First Baptist Church without anyone falling off one of the sides. There is a podium set up on the stage. A truck is backed up to one side of the stage with a large number of boxes showing through the partially rolled up back door.

It looks like all of Perry has turned out. It is a very somber crowd. Everyone is worried about what is going down. This is the first time that I know of that someone has called this kind of meeting so it has to be something big. Mayor McKinley has started tapping on the microphone and people start to draw in closer.

"Hello everyone. Can everyone hear me okay? I know it's very cold out here so we will try to make this as short as possible but it's going to take a while so please bear with us. Save any questions or comments until the end. We have asked everyone to gather here today so we can try to bring you up to date and pass on what little information we have about the power and communication outages. We also want to help everyone prepare for what's next if things continue as they are.

As most of you know on Christmas Eve we suffered what appeared to be a power outage. Most of you here have farms and are used to an occasional power outage and you were prepared for this with generators and kerosene lamps etc. Your biggest concern is will you have enough fuel to last until the outage is over.

Well this outage is now in its third day, some of you are running low on fuel and you want to know how much longer is this going to last. Well do to the fact that the outage has taken down most forms of communication, information and answers are very hard to come by. But I will give you what I've got.

The most recent update I've received from the capital in Oklahoma City is, to say the least, very disturbing. According to some top government officials this outage was not caused by something getting overloaded or frozen or anything of the sort but was caused by a deliberate act of one or more individuals.

Right now they are calling it a cyber-terrorist attack against the United States and its allies. This attack has completely brought down the infrastructure of not only the U.S. but it looks like most of the world.

It appears to have been some sort of computer virus that was launched somewhere in the U.S. As soon as it entered our Internet and intranet system it spread like sunshine on a clear day. It totally brought down the nation's infrastructure in less than 18 minutes."

The crowed starts mumbling and talking to each other. A loud voice erupts from the crowed and asks the question.

"How can a computer virus take down all our power?"

The Mayor yells into the mike to get people to settle down.

"Please! Please! Let me go on. Thanks. If you are like me and tolerate computers more than embrace them, then you are wondering how this could be. How can a computer virus kill my TV, my power, my radios, and most of all the power grid and communications?

I know of a few families with new cars that can't even get them to start. To try and shed some light on the subject I've asked Dr. Tom Harvey from the computer science department at O.U. To come here today and give us a possible explanation."

"As the Mayor stated I'm with the computer science department at O.U. I was asked to come here to try and explain how it might be possible for a computer virus to affect seemingly unrelated things like our electrical power, communications, etc.

I'm here to try and give you some insight and show you, that it is indeed possible for a computer virus, to cause the events of the last couple of days. I doubt anyone here would argue about the fact that we as a society have become more and more dependent on our computers, cell phones, iPads, etc. Especially the Internet.

Even here in the small town of Perry if you go through the drive through window at McDonald's, when you place your order, you are actually talking to someone setting in a cubicle in Omaha or in some cases Ethiopia. How does that happen? The

Internet. You buy gas at your local gas station, swipe your card and pay for it. How does that happen? The Internet.

In the last 10 years we have become more and more dependent on, and less and less aware of, the fact that we need the Internet in some shape or fashion to carry on our daily lives. In the last five years Congress has actually passed laws and organizations like the FCC have mandated rules that have forced people to become more dependent.

For example Congress said that by 2009 all full power analog TV stations had to stop broadcasting. Why? Because they use too much energy and now we were moving into the digital age. Now, TV stations use computers to prepare their content, store the content, and then push that content up to a satellite that uses a computer to transmit it digitally to your new flat screen TV that uses a microprocessor to translate it into the picture you see on the screen.

So what happens if you eliminate the computer or microprocessor? Your 52" flat screen TV is now a very expensive wall hanging that won't even light up. The same thing with you digital radios, your home alarm system, and now your car has to communicate via satellite to some computer somewhere to make sure you are supposed to be driving it. The list goes on and on and yes it even includes the power grid.

Power generating plants whether they are coal, steam, or nuclear, use computers in their control rooms to control and monitor the generators. If the computers go down the generators go down. At least until the redundant backup system kicks in or until the computer gets fixed.

What should happen, is once the computer fails, the redundant systems should take over, if that fails it should switch to a different generation plant that has detected the failure via the Internet or the power company's point to point connection.

Why that hasn't happened, I don't know. I find it hard to believe that all the redundant systems failed. It's almost like all their computers have failed, but that is really inconceivable. I'm sure they will get things back up, computers re-booted or whatever; I'm just here to give you a possible scenario of what could be happening.

Now, if this has indeed happened then we have really big problems. That being said I would like to bring up our next person to speak and she is going to explain the trouble we are in and that trouble is far greater than not being able to watch TV."

Dr. Harvey turns to exit the podium and the Mayor starts to get up and approach the podium when he is pushed aside by a lady that appears to be tired of listening to all this. She steps up to the microphone and addresses the crowed.

"My name is Maria Clark. I'm with the Federal Emergency Management Agency. I'm the one that called for this meeting here today. I called it because, as the professor stated we may have a much bigger problem. Obviously, the longer this outage goes on the worse things are going to get. I'm not going to sugar coat this thing. I'm here today to inform you of the fact that if this goes on, Perry Oklahoma, as well as every farming community in the country will be a very dangerous place to live."

This causes quite a stir in the crowed, which seems to irritate Maria even more.

"Please, hello, please, if you give me a moment I'll explain." She says. "Most of you are farmers. The power outage has caused you problems and in most cases you have found a way to work around them. But tonight at supper you will set down to a nice meal consisting of mostly things you have grown right on your own land. Unfortunately a completely different scenario is unfolding sixty miles down the road in Oklahoma City and other major cities around the country.

Due to the fact that their refrigerators stopped working three days ago, any food that was in it has spoiled. They can't go to the grocery store and get more because the grocery store, if they can find one that's open, has the same problem. No refrigeration.

So you say there are canned foods etc., that don't require refrigeration and they can get by on that until this is fixed. The only problem with that is that they can't pay for it. 95% of them have no cash. They have a little plastic card that is connected to their bank by way of the Internet. It is now just a piece of plastic.

If they go to the bank to draw their money out, they can't. Their account is nothing more than a bunch of data sitting on a computer somewhere. So in order to feed their kids they are just going to forcibly take the food. What happens when the shelves are empty? They are going to head north to a place where they actually grow the food. In this case that's Perry.

Now here again they aren't going to have any money and I'm sure most of you are very caring people and want to help some of these people feed their families. So you will gladly help them out. That's the way most country folk are. But, what happens when the number reaches the point to where it's taking the food out of your own family's mouth. Then the time for helping will be over and then you are going to protect your own. You have food and they want it. You will protect what's yours anyway you can. That's human nature.

I'm here to let you know that the government is going to assist you during this time. We will be setting up a temporary communications site right here on Delaware street in the old McLellan building.

Those of you that have farms that produce food and those of you that has dairy farms that produce milk, will be given two-way radios. This will allow you to communicate with our command center as well as emergency services. You will also receive up to date information on what's going on in your area via these radio.

When we wrap up here those of you that qualify should come up here to the bandstand with your I.D. and we will issue you a radio. Due to the limited number we will only be able to issue one radio per farm so don't ask for more. That's it."

She turns and walks away from the podium. People try to yell out questions but no one on the podium responds.

CHAPTER FOUR

WHO DO YOU TRUST

I walk into the kitchen where my mother is standing in front of the stove, steam is rising up from a pot on top of the stove and my mom reaches down and removes some fresh bread from the oven. Harlan is setting at the kitchen table reading a book. He moves his book over to keep it in a beam of sunlight coming from an overhead window. All the curtains are wide open and tied back. Sun streaming through the windows is the only illumination in the house.

"Mom, have you talked to Shane's mom lately?" I ask.

"Not since Christmas day."

"Weird."

"Why's that?" Mom asks.

"Well I didn't see him or any of his family at the square yesterday."

"There were thousands of people there; wouldn't it have been weirder if you had seen him?"

"Well his favorite thing at the park is the Hopes and Dreams Statue. We kind of have this thing that we started when we were little, that if one of us goes to the square for a carnival or something we check the statue to see if the other one is there. If they are not hanging around the statue then we leave a note telling where we are going to be. I left a note but he never took it."

"Abby, things are in turmoil. People were packed into the square. He probably couldn't get to the statue or his parents made him stay with them because of the crowd." Mom says.

"Well I really need to talk to him. Can we drive down to his house and see if they are home?"

"Sure. Later on this afternoon we will drive over there. I'm sure everything is fine. Well, as fine as they can be under the circumstances." Mom says.

"Mom, can I tell you something that's really bad and you not go berserk like you usually do?"

"Sure. If it's something bad you <u>have</u> to tell me."

"Promise you want get all freaky."

"Yes."

"The last time I talked to Shane was Christmas day when they came over."

"Ok."

"He told me that he had caused the power outage."

"Shane said he caused the power outage? And you believe him."

"I didn't at first. I couldn't stop laughing long enough. But then he told me about this computer virus that he had come up with that would do exactly what everyone is now saying happened. He even demonstrated it on Erica's computer."

"Sweetheart he was just playing games with you. He is a very smart boy and he just took what the sheriff was saying and made it into a scenario with him as villain."

"Well, the problem with your scenario is the sheriff showed up after he told me about it. How did he make it up if he hadn't heard it yet?"

"Very simple. The sheriff went to their house before he came here. As a matter of fact about two hours before he came here.

That's why him and his mother came over here. She wanted to tell me what the sheriff said and to see what I thought about it."

"That jackass! I can't believe he did that. What a liar!"

"I'm sure he was just trying to impress you." Mom says.

"Impress me? Do you know how freaked out I've been."

"That brings up and interesting point. You have believed since Christmas day that Shane started this fiasco and you are just now telling me. Why didn't you tell me as soon as you heard it?" Mom says.

"I don't know I guess deep down I really didn't believe he actually was the cause of it. Besides you know how irresponsible us twelve year olds are."

"Well if you had of told me sooner you wouldn't have been stressing out all this time." Mom says.

"I'm going to kill him."

"Well, while you're plotting his demise go down to the cellar and get some corn and whatever else you guys want for supper tonight. We can drive over to their house in a little while and you can kill him then." Mom says.

"Oh I'm gonna."

"Abby, just remember he made this stuff up because he likes you. He was just trying to impress you." Mom says.

"Oh I'm impressed all right."

The drive to Shane's house is short. Most of the time we just walk down there, but now there is a lot of snow on the ground and the temperature has dropped into the twenties.

Shane's parents are both really into the whole green thing. Shane's dad is an electronics engineer and a sort of inventor type guy. This coupled with the whole green thing makes their home quite an adventure sometimes. Solar panels, windmills, and large storage tanks are scattered all over their farm. In the past a lot of the town folks had made fun of the farm and how ugly all the contraptions made the place. But I bet now, with the temperature down in the twenties and the lack of power everywhere, the people were wishing their farms were as well equipped.

We pull up to the front gate, which for some reason is standing wide open.

"That's weird I've never seen their gate standing open like that." Mom says.

"It's probably due to the power thing." I said.

"They have been off the grid for years and it was always closed. The grid being down wouldn't affect anything on this farm. As a matter of fact they told your dad if he wanted he could run a cable across the pasture and connect our house to their system." Mom says.

As we followed the driveway up to the house mom brought up how pretty the yard was with the blanket of snow that was covering everything. We got out of the car and walked to the front door.

Usually by this time Shane's dog Zea greeted us. Zea didn't like strangers and was a good guard dog but he was always glad to see me because I always had a treat for him. Shane always said if someone wanted to rob the place all they would have to do is bring treats and Zea would hold the door open for them.

But today no Zea. Mom rang the doorbell and we waited. No response. So she rang it again. Still no response.

"Maybe it's broke." Mom says.

Then she banged on it real hard with her hand. Still no response.

"That's weird." Mom said.

"Both cars are under the carport. So they should be here. Maybe they're around back or something."

"It's twenty degrees I don't think they are having a barbecue." I said.

Mom tried the door but it was locked.

"Well let's look around and see where they are."

"Mom, as you pointed out when we pulled in, everything is covered by a blanket of snow. It hasn't snowed since Christmas night. No one has been in or out or walked around since then or there would be tracks. This also backs up my story of them not being at the square for that meeting.

28

Maybe Shane's virus grew wings and they flew out. Don't you have keys to their house mom?"

"Yes, but just for emergencies."

"Uh, they are obviously home and aren't coming to the door. Its twenty degrees out here so I officially declare this an emergency."

Mom digs through her purse and pulls out a ring full of keys.

"What's with all the keys?" I ask.

"This is my emergency keys. I have keys for several of the farms around here. You know, that are our friends. They all have keys to our house. If an emergency comes up we can assist each other if necessary."

Mom puts the key in the lock and pushes the door open.

"Hello any one here. Hello Joslyn. Hello Hank. Anyone here?"

No response. We made our way into the house and continued to yell hoping someone would respond. It was nice and warm in the house. The Christmas tree lights were blinking and what appeared to be the dishes from Christmas dinner were setting in the sink. I started up the stairs to check Shane's room. Mom told me to wait.

"Maybe you shouldn't go up there." Mom says.

"Mom, Shane won't care if I go in his room."

"That's not what I mean. Something isn't right here and I'm scared of what you might find up there. Let's drive into Perry and tell the sheriff what we have found."

"That's cool, but I'm checking Shane's room first."

"Wait for me." Mom says.

Mom followed me up the stairs. Shane's door was closed so I knocked on it.

"Shane you in there?"

No response. I pushed the door open but I closed my eyes because I was afraid of what I might see. I slowly opened my eyes and looked around. No Shane lying on the bed dead. That was a relief. Everything looked normal. Dirty clothes strewn all over the floor, open books lying around on his desk.

"Looks like it was the maid's year off." I said.

Mom walked out to check the other rooms. I noticed the CD rom drive light flicker on his computer. That's strange. Why isn't his computer dead? I walked over to it and moved the mouse. The screen lit up. His screen background was that of a large Monarch Butterfly with its wings extended. I pushed the eject key on the keyboard and ejected the CD that was in the drive. I quickly put the CD in my coat pocket before mom came back in the room. I don't know why I took the CD but I just felt I needed to hide it for some reason. Mom walked back in the room.

"Everything looks normal. Their bed is made up and nothing looks out of place." Mom says.

"Except for them," I said.

"Let's just assume that they left with someone else and somehow the snow covered their tracks."

"Have you ever known of them to take Zea with them anywhere?" I ask.

"Zea could be outside in the barn and hasn't come out because it's so cold." Mom said.

"So I'll walk back there and see."

"No I don't think you should." Mom said. "I don't think we should disturb anything."

I turned and looked on Shane's printer and there was a picture he had printed out of Zea with a big red circle with a line through it.

"Oh wow. I forgot. Shane told me that those guys took Zea and had posted a picture of him on line."

"I think we should get in the car and go get the sheriff." Mom said.

"Fine, but you are going to be really embarrassed when you find out they are all in the barn." I said.

They walk out the front door and re-lock it. They get in the car and drive off to get the sheriff.

As we pull up to the sheriff's office it seemed weird. The sheriff's office is right across from the town square. There is always a ton of people milling around. There are at least two guys always setting in front of the Courthouse playing checkers even when it's freezing cold. Now there is no one. The park is empty, the streets have no cars, and it's like a ghost town. Usually by this time there would be a lot of preparations being made for the New Year's Eve celebration but there was nothing.

As we go into the sheriff's office I could hear generators sputtering behind the building and the lights in the office began to flicker.

"Excuse me folks," one of the deputies said as he tried to get out as we came in. "I have to put some fuel in the generators I'll be right back."

The sheriff came up to the front desk.

"Good evening Angela what brings you out during all this? Is everything ok?"

"Not really." Mom says.

"We were wondering if you know where the Bevil's might be."

"The Bevil's," the sheriff replies.

"Yes, we just went over to their farm and they are nowhere to be found. Their cars are all in the carport. Their power is up but we can't find them."

The sheriff continues to ask a lot of questions and started filling out a report.

"I'll head over there and take a look around. I'm sure everything is ok, but I'll check it out just to make sure. I'll drop by your place if I find out anything."

CHAPTER FIVE

WE'RE HERE TO HELP

M om and I are setting at the kitchen table talking with my dad about what was going on with Shane and his family. Harlan is lying on the floor working on an electronics kit. There is a knock at the door and Harlan jumps up and answers it.

"Dad there's someone at the door."

Dad walks over to the door. Standing outside is Maria Clark and two men. One is in a business suite and the other in a camouflaged military uniform.

"Hello Mr. Tate." Maria says as she sticks out her hand to shake dad's hand. "I don't know if you remember me, but I was the one that spoke at the town meeting a couple of days ago."

"Sure dad says," as he shakes her hand. "Please come in its awful cold out there."

Maria turns and introduces the two men as they start to enter the house.

"This is Steve Hill. He works with me at F.E.M.A. and this is Lieutenant Colonel Krom who is with a special task force appointed by the president to be a liaison between the town's people, F.E.M.A., and the Military."

"Military?" Dad says.

"Yes, do you have a place we could maybe sit down and talk for a minute?"

Mom and I get up and mom says, "Here y'all sit here."

Dad introduces mom and I and then they sit down at the table. Harlan and I move to the den and set down on the couch.

"Mr. Tate I'm going to be as straight forward about this as I can. I don't sugar coat things and I want you to understand that anything I say here is fact."

"Sure." Dad says.

"First, I want you to understand that not only our country but countries all over the world are experiencing something that no one, no matter how hard we tried, could have prepared for. We are facing a situation and a crisis that is well, like no other we, as a nation has ever faced. One that neither our government nor any of the other governments around the world are prepared to handle. With all the years of planning and preparing no one planned for the exact scenario that has taken place."

"Surely you people have planned on the possibility of the Internet going down and taking down power and communication." Dad said.

"That's very true. There are all kinds of plans in place for that. None of them or none of the people that makes these plans ever thought that it was possible for the network to go down and stay down. All these plans figured it would be down for a few days at most a week. No one planed on all of it, ever being down.

The government has spent billions of dollars making sure that it could not go down. But that's all irrelevant now. It's down and from the last reports I received it looks like it isn't coming back up. At least in the form that it was in."

"Are you telling me that it can't be fixed. That's the dumbest thing I ever heard. We have some of the smartest people in the world in this country. People who invented all this crap to start with. You telling me they can't re-boot all those computers or replace the ones that are broke and bring it back up?" Dad asks.

"Let me explain what's going on." Maria says.

"The computer virus that caused all this, we are calling it the <u>Monarch</u> virus, as it propagated."

I interrupt Maria in mid-sentence.

"What did you say they are calling it?" I ask.

"The Monarch Virus". Maria says.

"Where did they get that name?" I ask.

"I'm not sure. Actually I asked where they came up with that name and told them I thought it was a lame name for such an evil thing and they told me that it was named after the Monarch Butterfly because of the butterfly effect whatever that is."

I look at my mom with a very shocked look on my face. Maria continues on.

"As I was saying, this virus as it propagated, destroyed each computer that it connected to."

Dad says, "Ok so they replace those computers and it's fixed." Dad says.

"The only problem with that is it's still out there. It has embedded itself in satellites, routers, firewalls, and every other network device and no one can figure out how it did it or how to get rid of it. Any new computer that is started up works fine until you try to connect it to any network that was in existence on Christmas day." Maria says.

"So you build a whole new network." Dad says.

"That will take years and billions of dollars and with the millions of devices out there just one, infected one, gets plugged into the new network and we are right back to square one."

"Ok so what does all this have to do with us?" Dad asks.

"Well, with limited communications, you probably are not aware of how bad things have become in the big cities. There is rioting, looting, people being killed for the food they had on their kitchen table. It is total chaos and it is happening at a rate that no one thought it would or planned for."

"I can't believe all this." Dad says.

"The government is trying to maintain law and order with curfews and try to limit people from leaving their homes but that has zero effect on hungry people. So what we are doing now is building temporary camps to help house and feed people. House the injured and sick ones, and feed all of them.

We are trying to locate these camps close to the food supplies and on major roads to make them easier to get to. Your farm has a lot of property that backs up to and runs alongside Interstate 35. It's ideal for a campsite. Would you allow the government to build a camp on your property?"

"Well I'm not sure. What all does this involve, what are you going to do to the property and will it be returned to its original condition when they leave."

Steve assures dad that it will be taken care of then Maria jumps in.

"Mr. Tate it would be nice if you would accommodate us on this but to be quite frank we are going to do it whether you agree or not.

We have to consider the needs of the many and not the few."

"Then why are you here?" Dad says.

"We wanted to inform you of what we were going to do and try to get you on board with the plan. It's a lot easier to have an agreeable partner than an enemy in something like this."

"Sure, you can use the property." Dad says.

"I'm willing to help people out any way I can."

"Great." Maria says.

"You will see trucks begin to unload materials out there as early as tomorrow morning."

"You are sure the government will put everything back like they found it when they are finished?" Dad says.

"I'm sure it will be even better when they are done." Maria says.

"There is one other thing you should know. The military police will also be out at this camp. Some of the units we put in will actually be holding cells. Obviously there are a lot of people who break the law in times like this. The local jail here only has four small cells and we would fill that up very quickly so we have to make some temporary arrangements.

Remember that most of the people we will be detaining out there are not hardened criminals they are just people that in a lot of cases were trying to feed their kids. So they break into some ones house or forcibly take what they need from someone.

Unfortunately there are those that will try to take advantage of this crisis and use it to justify stealing what they want whether they need it or not. We have to deal with them as well as send a message to everyone else that the law is the law and we will not tolerate those kinds of actions."

With that they stood and excused themselves.

"Dad, are you really ok with them putting that stuff out there?" I ask.

"Not really, but what are you going to do? It's like the woman said they were going to do it even if I didn't go along with it."

"That's just not right." I said. "I'm all for feeding the people and giving them medical treatment and stuff but putting a prison out there is scary."

"It will be ok so don't worry about it." Dad says.

"Right. They build a makeshift prison out of substandard portable buildings and fill them with very angry and dangerous people. And where are those people going to run to and try to hide when they break out of this cracker box of a jail. Right, the nearest farm to them, and where would that be, oh yes, that would be ours. Nothing to worry about there."

"Have I told you how much you have started to sound like your mother lately?" Dad says.

"Well she's right." Mom says.

"I know. We are just going to have to be very careful and watch what's going on around here very closely." Dad says.

"Well, at least we know that they have Shane and he has told them about the virus." I said. "Because that Maria woman talked about the Monarch Virus and the only place they could have got that is from Shane."

"Well if they have him then we know he's ok. Right, if they aren't keeping him in one of their makeshift prisons." I said.

"I'm sure they're not." Mom says.

"What I don't understand is, if they have got the information from him then, why haven't they released him?" I ask.

"They probably have him trying to come up with a fix." Dad says.

Dad gets up and comes over to me and puts his arms around me.

"I know you're worried about your friend but you have to slow down a little. I'm sure he's ok. It's not some terrorist that has him; it's the good guys. He will be back home before you know it." Dad says.

"I hope your right." I said.

"Mom do you think this will change Shane?" I ask.

"What do you mean?" Mom asks.

"Well Shane has always been a real sensitive kind of guy. It's one of the things I really like about him, but I think this will destroy him."

"He didn't do it on purpose so why would it bother him?"

"It doesn't matter if he didn't mean to do it, actually that will probably make it worse, but according to the rumors there are already thousands of people that have died because of this, and no matter how you look at it Shane caused it. This time in history, when one of the biggest tragedies to hit the world, is recorded, it will be recorded that it was because of a twelve-year-old boy from Perry Oklahoma named Shane Bevil."

"You're not worried about the government having him; you're worried about what he may do to himself." I start crying and say, "Yes."

"Abby listen to me mom says, Shane will be ok. He is a very smart kid. He would never do anything like that. He loves his mom and dad too much to do anything that would hurt them.

His mom and dad are with him and they will help him through this. So promise me you won't worry about that anymore?"

"I can't promise you that."

"Well at least promise me when you start thinking like that you will come and talk to your dad or I about it. We're here for you and want to help."

CHAPTER SIX

FIRST SUNDAY

It's Sunday morning and mom, Harlan and I are setting at the kitchen table having breakfast when dad walks into the kitchen.

"Morning everyone."

There are vague mumblings saying good morning returned from all three of them.

"I heard today that the military has set up some kind of temporary facility out at the Warren Ranch. Jerry Johnson, the foreman out there at the ranch came by early this morning to pick up some feed corn and he told me about the place and said he swears he saw the Bevil family being escorted into the building just before dawn a few days ago. He didn't know what this facility was, but said it had a lot of generators and power type equipment connected to it." Dad says.

"Well we need to go out there and see them." I said.

"He said he wasn't absolutely sure it was them and he said whatever they are doing out there, they definitely don't want anyone interrupting them because it is heavily guarded and no one is allowed in or out without permission."

"But dad, Shane has to be out there. This explains what happened to him and his mom and dad. They found out that he was the one that caused all of this and they arrested him."

"Abby, just chill for a moment. If Shane had anything to do with all of this, which I don't believe for one second that he did, but let's just say what he told you was true. He didn't do it intentionally. I mean he didn't maliciously inject a virus into the Internet to take down; He was just trying to retaliate to the three boys that took his dog. They aren't going to arrest him for that. I'm sure they would give him a lot of grief over it, but not arrest him or even hold him against his will. This is still America you know. Besides he's only twelve years old."

"So why are they holding him out there then?" I said.

"We don't know for sure that they are and if for some nut-so reason this were true then they are probably hiding him because ninety percent of the world would love to see him strung up."

"Look dad, Shane and his parent's just disappeared. Nowhere to be found. Even the sheriff doesn't know where they are and has been looking all over for them. Now we have some man and woman with a young boy staying out at some mysterious government facility. Connect the dots dad. It's not rocket science."

"But don't you think if that were true that the sheriff would know about it?"

"The sheriff is one of us." I said. "They aren't going to tell him anything."

"He's one of us?" Dad says.

"Yes, we are the mindless town's people, they are the all-knowing government, and they aren't going to tell us anything. All they are going to say is, we know what's best for you."

"Abby don't even go there! Don't start with the whole secret government conspiracy and F.E.M.A death camps, end of the world stuff. This is really not a good time to be talking that nonsense."

"Said the man that just gave <u>F.E.M.A.</u> permission to build a <u>camp</u> on his property." I said.

"Abby, shut up! I'm not in any mood to hear this crap, so knock it off. This is not some Internet blog or Disney movie, this is reality so let it go."

"Ok, but can we drive out there to see for ourselves what's going on?"

Mom jumps in and says; "Sure we will go by there when we get out of church."

"Fine, dad says. But just understand when we use up the gasoline that we have it may be a long time before we get anymore."

Later we left and drove to church. The drive was very quiet because no one wanted to talk about what they were thinking. When we finally got there, the church parking lot was full of cars. A small area is blocked off and has tables set up with foodstuff, stacked up, and being handed out to those that are in need.

For the first time in over two weeks the sun was visible in the sky and the temperature was up above freezing. It was good to see my friends. My best friend is Molly and she was standing in front of my Sunday school classroom waiting for me to show up. As we grabbed each other and hugged you would have thought we hadn't seen each other in years. It was good to finally communicate with someone my own age. Someone that is from the same world that I am from.

We went in and as always found a place to sit so we could sit by each other. Our Sunday school teacher was a super nice lady named Amy. She made class a lot of fun and everyone wanted to be in her class.

After the class, and as we were leaving, Ms. Amy stopped me on the way out and asked me where Shane was.

"He never misses, and I was just wondering if he was sick or something."

"I don't know where he is. We went by his house and no one was there." I said.

"He's probably gone somewhere for the holidays." Amy says.

"I think he would have told me if they had plans to do that." I said.

"Well I hope everything is Ok." Amy says.

Molly and I walked into the auditorium and went to our normal place to sit.

"Molly, I think there is something really weird going on with Shane." As I began telling her the story Pastor Gleason started talking.

"It's good to see everyone here this morning. I wasn't sure what kind of crowd we would have here this morning. I know, with the circumstances we have all been subjected to in the last few days that coming to church is probably not high on your list of priorities but you're here and that is a good thing.

God said "Where many are gathered in my name, then there will I be in the midst."

There has never been a time, at least in my lifetime, where we needed Him more than we do today.

We have kind of been thrown back to the days of yesteryear where the church was not only a place to come and learn about God but a place to find out how your neighbors were doing and you could even see and hear what information the visitors coming in from other towns and places had to share. During that time, and now at this time, the church was and still can be a great asset to our community by being a place to bring your extra food and water so it can be distributed to those in need.

But more importantly it was, and is, a place that we can come together and call on God for his wisdom and guidance.

Now as most of you know I'm an avid ham radio operator. I have always said that Ham Radio still has a place in this modern computerized world in which we live. Well now people can see what I was talking about.

With the help of the solar powered electrical equipment that Mr. Bevil gave me, both the Church and my home are able to function pretty well during the power outage. One of the benefits to having that solar power is that I've been able to fire up my radio and help several families here in town get in contact with their family members in other parts of the country.

I've also been able to hear firsthand how some of the other areas in our country have been devastated by the lack of food and water. How rioting and looting" . . .

A man stands up at a point near the front of the church and cuts Pastor Gleason off mid-sentence. I recognized him as Colonel Krom from his visit to the house.

"Pastor Gleason, I hate to interrupt you right in the middle of your message, and I beg the forgiveness of you and your congregation, but I need to stop you from going on with the information you are giving out."

"What? What do you mean? Who are you?"

"I'm Sorry; I'm Lieutenant Colonel Krom. I'm with a special task force appointed by the president and I'm here to try and help people get through this situation that we are in. Pastor Gleason, the problem is that no one has any way to verify the information that you have heard so we don't know if it's accurate, miss-construed, or even fabricated. The country is like a powder keg right now and it would be very easy for someone in your position to pass on a rumor that effects someone in the wrong way and literally light's the fuse that will cause that powder keg to explode. The riots that you are speaking of for the most part were caused by such miss-information."

"I understand your concern but couldn't you have come to me before services and discussed this with me?" Pastor Gleason said.

"Yes I could have, and I would have if I had known about your access to a Ham Radio and that there was a possibility of you passing on information that you picked up from the radio, I would have talked to you about this earlier. I'm sorry that I didn't please forgive me."

"But the people setting here want to hear about what's happening in the world." Pastor Gleason said. "We have been in the dark for over a week."

"I understand that, but you have to understand that I can't allow you to continue spreading this information until we've had a chance to look at it and verify its validity."

"So what exactly does that mean?" Pastor Gleason asks.

"It means that you can stand up there and talk about God, sing hymns, and teach the Bible all you want to. But you can't talk about the things you <u>hear</u> over the radio unless it's been cleared by my office."

"Colonel you are treading in some very treacherous waters there. I understand to a certain existent what you are telling me and I will try and work with your office in the future and notify you of what I <u>will</u> be talking about at the next service. If you have some kind of proof that something is bogus then I will do what you ask and not speak of it from the pulpit. Please understand that you will not control what comes from this pulpit. I will speak and teach whatever I feel God would have me to speak and teach."

"Pastor Gleason there is no need to get spun up about this and to get everyone mad. I'm not here to violate anyone's first amendment rights. I came here today to hear your message and I would love to hear the rest of it. Minus those things you picked up on your radio."

"I'm going to ask our assistant Pastor John Tubb to come up here and continue on with the service while the Colonel and I go into my office and discuss this matter further." Pastor Gleason says.

John Tubb starts making his way to the pulpit as Pastor Gleason steps down and walks down the Aisle toward the back doors of the church. The Colonel joins him and they walk out. There is a great commotion in the church as people start voicing their opinion on what has taken place.

After about forty-five minutes of improv preaching brother Tubb is ready to close the service. Pastor Gleason walks back into the auditorium and stands at the back waiting for brother Tubb to wrap up. As everybody is starting to stand Pastor Gleason walks to the pulpit and asked for everyone's attention.

"I know everyone is ready to leave but I wanted to take a few minutes to fill you in on what I discussed with that colonel that interrupted the service earlier. First off, don't anyone be misled by his comments that he was just here like everybody else to hear the message. The fact is, he and others like him, are attending church services all around the country to see what is being said by the preachers and pastor in regard to the crisis we are facing.

It seems that the government is very concerned about the communications that are transpiring around the country especially in the rural areas like ours. I can understand his point and I can even see where making sure of the validity of some report before you pass it on would help to keep everyone correctly informed. That being said I'm not sure if I agree with their methods.

I was just told that the Colonel or someone like him would be attending all our services to make sure we abide by these <u>rules</u> and if we don't we will be <u>stopped</u> from saying anything from the pulpit. I couldn't get him to elaborate on what exactly they tend to do to <u>stop</u> someone but he made it clear that I didn't want them to <u>stop</u> me from preaching. Now I certainly want to abide by the law or any temporary rules that the government inflicts on us during this time. But as always I will say and preach on whatever God puts on my heart.

However, if I understand it right and according to the Colonel, the concern is what I say from the <u>pulpit</u>. So I see no problem with any of you coming by my office or after the service asking me what I've heard. I will be more than happy to share with anyone those things that other people like myself are hearing and seeing around the world and report on the ham radio. That being said I wish all of you the best and we will see you next Sunday."

I asked Molly if she could possibly come over to the house and maybe spend the night. We cleared it with our parents and headed out to the car. I explained to Molly that we were going to run by the Warren Ranch on the way home to see if there really was a military facility out there and if there were, if they would tell us what was going on inside.

CHAPTER SEVEN

THE WARREN RANCH

The Warren ranch is a very beautiful, very large, ranch that raises the most beautiful Quarter Horses in the world. My grandpa grew up with George the son that now owns the ranch. I learned how to ride a horse there and dad bought my horse, Zoe, from the Warrens when I was only six years old. Every time my Girl Scout troop goes on an overnight camping trip it is always out here at the ranch so over the years it has become one of my favorite places to go.

But, the trip out to the ranch today seemed like it was taking forever. The snow was starting to melt and so the roads were all slushy and the snow chains on the tires were hitting the asphalt and made an awful noise.

Finally we made the turn to pull into the ranch. To the right and just inside the entrance a new razor wire fence had been put in place and it stretched down the driveway and up to the house. Behind the fence was a pair of modular buildings and as the foreman had said they had a lot of generators, antennas, and two fairly large dish shaped antennas. There was a gate in the middle of the fence and there was a guard sitting in a Humvee and one standing by the gate. Beside the modular buildings was an area marked as a helipad and beside it were several large fuel tanks.

I leaned forward and whispered to mom

"That's how they did it".

"What, what are you talking about?" Mom said.

"The helipad. That's why there were no tracks at Shane's house. They used a helicopter to take him away." I said.

"Ok Nancy Drew let's try not to turn this into one of your who-dun-its. Besides they live right by us don't you think that we would have heard a helicopter land at their house?"

"Maybe we weren't home when they did it. All I'm saying is that explains why there are no tracks coming into or leaving their house." I said.

"Ok I'll give you that. There weren't any tracks and that would explain that but I think you are letting your imagination run away." Mom said.

Dad pulled the car on down to the house. As we started getting out of the car I noticed a car pulling up to the gate and being waved in by the guard. The car pulled up to the front entrance of one of the modular buildings and the driver got out. I grabbed dad by the arm and said:

"Dad, look that's that Colonel Krom that was at the house and then at the church."

"Wow, it sure is. He seems to get around quite a bit."

Dad turns and started walking toward the fence and the colonel.

"Hey, Colonel:" Dad yelled.

The colonel turned and saw dad and started walking toward him. Molly and I ran and caught up with dad and we met the colonel at the fence.

"Good afternoon Mr. Tate. Didn't expect to see you out here." The Colonel says.

"The Warrens are old family friends and we wanted to come out and see how they were doing." Dad says.

"Well, they aren't actually here. I guess Mrs. Warren was really concerned about her mother down in Texas so they decided to try and drive down and check on her."

"Really. Do you know what part of Texas they were going to because I heard it was really getting bad around the Dallas area?" Dad says.

"Not sure but I think they said College Station, and as far as I know everything is pretty peaceful there and in the Dallas area. See, that's what I was trying to get people to see at your church earlier. Miss-Information. The fact is everything is going pretty well in Texas yet somewhere you heard right the opposite. The Warrens may have heard the same thing and decided to take the risk of trying to drive down there."

"What are you doing out here?" I asked.

"Well as the F.E.M.A agent explained to your father at your house the other day, we are setting up camps around the county to make food and medical services available to those who need it."

"This doesn't look like a camp designed to feed people." Molly says.

"It's not. This is a communication and command center that we set up to coordinate our efforts." The colonel said.

"I thought you set that up in town in the old McLellan building." Dad says.

"We decided that the McLellan space would serve better for food storage."

"I thought you said that the reason you were building the camps on our farms was so that you were close to the food source and wouldn't require any storage?" I said.

"May I ask why I'm getting the third degree here?" The colonel says.

"I'm sorry colonel; my daughter has recently became quite a conspiracy theorist."

"I just think it's strange." I said.

I am cut off by dad.

"That's enough Abby. You and Molly go back to the car."

"Please believe me Abby we are just here to help and for the time being you must let us decided what's best for you and your family." The Colonel says.

The ride back home was very quiet. Dad was very upset and said he didn't want to hear a peep out of me. Mom was just letting it slide she knows how to choose her battles with dad and figured this should be one that takes place when there were no witnesses around. Besides I don't think dad was just upset with me I think he was beginning to think I was right and that the colonel was out here for more than just feeding the hungry.

As we drove home we went over an overpass that crossed Interstate 35. Dad said, "Wow look at that."

We looked down on the Interstate and there were a lot of cars and trucks parked on the both sides of the road going in both directions. The majority of them were on the side that was coming into Perry.

"Where did all those come from?" I ask.

"I guess its people who ran out of gas and had to pull over." Dad said.

"But there are no people." I said.

"I guess they have been setting there for quite some time and the people ether got rides with passing cars or walked on in to town." Dad says.

"Wow things are getting really bad dad." I said.

"Yea it appears so."

"If they went into town I wonder where they are. We didn't see anybody walking around when we drove from the house to the church or from the church all the way to here. Looks like they just disappeared." I said.

It was creepy.

When we finally got to the house Molly and I headed straight to my room. Molly knew I was really bothered by what was going on and she tried to make me do other things to keep my mind off of it. I had never realized how much time we spent with computer related activities each day.

After the third board game I couldn't take it anymore and I drug Harlan's old Speak and Say out of his closet and we opened it up and started making it say things that it was not designed to say.

Molly and I have been friends since the first grade. She moved here from Las Vegas and we became the best of friends. We like exactly the same things. Same music, same movies, same cute guys. We also disliked the same things. Same foods, same teachers, Justin Beiber. She had spent the night here many times and I had spent the night at her house many times. We would make short whacked out videos. We would hide under the sheets with a flashlight and make up scary stories. But tonight was a lot different. We didn't have to make up a scary story because we were living in one.

"Molly you were best friends with Shane, what do you think happened to him?"

"Abby, don't say we <u>were</u> best friends. We <u>are</u> best friends. He's okay, nothing has happened to him."

"How can you be so sure?" I said.

"His mom and dad probably went to check on some of their family members who live in a different town or somewhere else." Molly says.

"Wrong! All their family members live here in Perry except for Shane's grandparents on his mother's side. That's why they moved back here."

"Ok, maybe one of them got sick and they are at the hospital." Molly says.

"Wrong! Sheriff checked that first thing."

"Ok, have you even been back over there since you and your mom went? He may have been at home all this time." Molly says.

"Wrong! My mom left a note at their house telling his mother we needed to see them as soon as they got back and we have heard nothing. Plus, my mom talked to sheriff Hardery yesterday and he said they were nowhere to be found."

"Abby, I just can't believe that the government kidnapped Shane and his parents and have them hid away somewhere." Molly says.

"Not somewhere, at the Warren Ranch." I said.

"Whatever. This is America the government can't just take you somewhere and keep you there if you don't want to be there. Maybe they volunteered to go somewhere with them. Maybe they are trying to help." Molly says.

"I'm not saying that the government kidnapped them and are going to "disappear" them forever. I'm just saying that the government has them and is holding them against their will." I said.

"If they know that Shane is the one that released the virus then they probably want him to come up with a way to undo it." Molly says.

"If that's the case then why take the whole family."

"He's twelve years old so they can't really arrest him." Molly says.

"I know that if he knew a way to undo all of this he would tell them how, so they wouldn't need to keep him for that. I'm sure their computer guys got him to show them how he created the virus and that would have only taken a few hours not days. So the only reason I can figure out is that they don't want anybody else to get a hold of him."

"Or, he is kind of weird about things sometime maybe he won't tell them anything and they are going to torture his parents in front of him until he tells them." Molly says.

"Ok you need to reel that imagination back in girl." I said.

"I wish we had a way to see what's on this CD." I said as I pulled the CD out of my coat.

"Where did you get that?" Molly asked.

"I took it out of Shane's computer when I was in his room. I don't know if he left it there for me to find or maybe it was something he was working on and then he had to leave in a hurry and he just forgot to eject it."

"Maybe it was a music CD he had burned and was listening to. Without a working computer there is no way to find out what's on it." Molly said.

"I have an older cd player at home, if it's a music CD we could tell easily." Molly says.

"But it's at your house where there is no electricity and we are staying at my house where the CD player isn't." I said.

"You know. I know where there is a working computer. Shane's house. At least it appeared to be working when I took this CD out of it. In the morning we will go for a nice horseback ride and ride over there and check it out. Of course they are probably watching his house and they will wonder what we are doing there."

"Wonderful, Molly says. "I get to ride on a frozen horse, break into a house, and probably get arrested or worse disappeared. You really know how to entertain company Abby Tate."

CHAPTER EIGHT

CHECK IT OUT

"Mom, Molly and I want to go horseback riding?"
"Are you nuts, its freezing cold outside and there's snow and ice all over the ground?" Mom says.

"The sun is out and the thermometer shows forty-two degrees. It'll be great. The horses need to get out of the barn."

"Check with your dad. Get him to saddle up the horses for you."

"K. Erica!" I yelled.

"What?" Erica yelled back.

"We are going to go riding and Molly is going to take Murdock."

"Whatever!"

"Dad!" I yelled.

"He's outside so stop yelling." Mom said.

We went outside and found dad at the barn.

"Dad can you help Molly put a saddle on Murdock?"

"You guys going for a ride. There is still a lot of snow on the ground." Dad says.

"We will stick to the roads and ride in the ruts." I said.

"Think about the horses. I know they are designed to handle the weather, but it's still cold and their hooves get cold. Don't be gone longer than an hour."

"Yes dad."

"And be careful, as you saw yesterday there are a lot of people walking around out there and they might try to get you to give them a ride or even try to take your horse. As a matter of fact be back in thirty minutes."

"Dad we'll be fine. I've ridden in the snow many times and if it will make you feel better we will ride across the pasture and stick to the foot trails."

"Yes, I think that would be better. If you see someone you don't know high tail it back here. Agreed?"

"Agreed."

"Also, while you're at Shane's house, if they are still gone, check on their livestock to see if they've been fed and watered. Henry has all that stuff set up to run automatically but it has to run out of feed sometime."

"What are you talking about?" I said. "What makes you think we were going by his house?"

"Come on, I know you and I know that you just didn't decide to go horseback riding this morning." Dad Said.

"So you are ok with it?" I said.

"I didn't say that, but here is your mother's key to their house. If anybody besides one of the Bevil's is there then leave. Don't talk to them, don't ask them what they are doing there, just leave. Ok?"

"OK."

With the temperature in the forties the horses were really frisky. Zoe wanted to take off and run and it was all I could do to keep her from doing it. Murdock on the other hand was quite content to stay in the barn where it was warm. Finally we got them both headed in the right direction and we were on our way.

Zoe knew the way to Shane's house very well and was ready to go see her true love, Shane's horse, Fat Biscuit, or Biscuit for short. Shane and I had got the horses at the same time and we had both learned how to ride them at the same time. Murdock seems to be really jealous of Biscuit and they were always trying to impress Zoe with their prancing around.

As we come to the top of the hill that overlooked the Bevil's farm everything looks peaceful. Looking up at a clear beautiful sky made it kind of hard to imagine that the world had suddenly and without notice come to a screeching halt. Wow, you definitely could never get your head around the possibility that a kid living in the picturesque farm down below caused it to happen.

As we approached the house everything looked normal just like it did when mom and I was here before. The snow was still pretty much intact but had started melting around the edges.

"Let's go around back. We can tie the horses up to the porch and they will be out of sight." I said.

As we rode around to the back of the house I looked around at the snow for signs or traces that someone had been here.

"Molly look at that." I said.

"What?"

We got off the horses and walked over to an area of the snow that appeared to have been disturbed.

"See that." I pointed to two long thin areas where the snow had been disturbed. "Doesn't it look like the skids of a helicopter could have made those two areas?"

"Well they are about the right size and shape." Molly says.

I took out my digital camera and took a few pictures to show to mom.

"Shouldn't we see if there is anyone at home?" Molly asks.

I walk up to the back door and knock. No response so I knocked harder. Still no response so I took out the key and opened the door.

"Anybody home?" I yelled as I opened the door.

"Hello, anybody here?"

We walk in and everything looked as it did before. Christmas lights still blinking and dishes in the sink.

"Molly, figure out how to turn those Christmas lights off." I said.

"I don't think we should touch anything." Molly said.

"We aren't burglars." I said.

"I'm sure they would appreciate us turning them off."

"What if they left them on for a reason?" Molly asked.

"They did. They were being taken by force and their captures were probably in a hurry and didn't think it was cool to stop and turn off the Christmas tree lights. Just turn them off. I'm going to see what's on this disk."

I walk into Shane's room followed close behind by Molly who didn't shut the lights off.

"It's gone."

"What's gone?" Molly asked.

"His computer. It was setting right there on his desk. Everything is gone, cd's, printer, monitor, USB drives. All that stuff was sitting right here on his desk and was even turned on. I guess they came back to get it."

"Let's get out of here." Molly says.

"Wow I can't believe it. Looks like they also got his clothes and stuff, which is a good thing."

"Why is that a good thing?" Molly asked.

"Well, if they had just taken his computer I would figure that they didn't want anyone to get a hold of it or they were destroying any evidence that could be used against them. By taking his clothes I figure he is still alive thus he needs his clothes and he requested his computer to use."

"My God, your mother was right when she called you Nancy Drew."

"Look around. Shane had a laptop that he brought to school sometimes; maybe it's still here."

Molly starts digging around in his closet and I look under the bed.

"Bingo!" Molly yells.

Sitting on the shelf under some magazines was his laptop.

"Ka Ching." I said.

Molly starts to open the lid and I yell, "Stop! We can't turn it on until we disable the wireless card and make sure it can't get to the Internet or any network. Assuming of course it's not already dead."

"This place is creeping me out I think we need to get out of here." Molly says.

"Ok but I'm taking the laptop. Shane won't care that I borrowed it."

I dig around in the closet and find a backpack and I stick the laptop in it.

"Let's boogie. Let's walk down to the barn and check on Biscuit."

We untie the horses and walk down to the barn. As we start getting close Zoe starts trying to run ahead and doesn't like the fact that I'm holding her back with the reins.

"Settle down girl. You know you are about to see your true love don't you."

As we get to the barn you can here Biscuit inside as he starts to snort and whinny as he senses them outside. I open the top half of the barn door and Biscuit immediately pokes his head out. I start to reach for him but I'm pushed out of the way by Zoe who is determined to get to Biscuit first.

"Would you settle down?

Here Molly hold Zoe's reins while I go in and check things out." I said.

I go into the barn and look around at the automatic feed and water troughs. Everything looks normal. I walk back outside.

"Everything looks normal in there. There is plenty of water and feed. The only problem is the poop is getting really deep. So obviously no one has been here in a while. I'm going to ask dad if we can come back and get Biscuit and bring him to our place until we find out what's going on." I said.

I close the barn door and we get on the horses and ride home. As we get to the house we notice the sheriff's car in the driveway.

"Well I wonder what he's doing here. Maybe he has news about Shane." I said.

"I hope your dad doesn't notice that you didn't have that backpack when you left." Molly said.

"Let's go around to the back and put the horses up. I'll leave the backpack in the barn until the coast is clear." I said.

We ride the horses around to the back and take the saddles off. I hide the backpack under some hay in the barn and we go into the house.

Dad and the Sheriff are setting at the kitchen table drinking coffee.

"Hey Sheriff Hardery what brings you over here? You have news about Shane?" I ask.

"Hey Abby, Molly, actually I do have some information. I was just telling your father that I had asked Colonel Krom if he could assist in finding out where Shane and his family were. This morning he came by the office and told me that the Bevil's were over in Enid. It appears that Shane's dad volunteered to help out with the relief efforts at Vance Air Force Base and since Joslyn's father and mother live there they are staying with them.

I guess they actually picked the Bevil's up with one of the rescue helicopter right at their house."

"See Abby I told you everything was fine." Dad said.

"Wow, that's cool. Did he happen to mention when they might be back?" I said.

"He said it shouldn't be much longer, they think they can start bringing the power up in a couple days." The sheriff said.

"Did he happen to mention when Shane's grandparents moved to Enid?" I asked. "When they were here right before Christmas Shane said they were still living in Tulsa."

"You know I thought they lived in Tulsa," the sheriff said. "Maybe the colonel got the city wrong anyway it's good to know they are ok. Now I've got to be moving on. I have to block the road this morning while they bring in all those portable buildings and diesel generators because they have to cross over the highway to get to your place. They told me they were seventy-five of them." The sheriff said.

"Seventy-five! Are they building a camp or a city?" Dad asked.

"I don't know the sheriff said but they are calling it Camp Hopkins and they said they would have it open in six days." The sheriff said.

"That's crazy. How can they set up that many buildings in six days? It would take hundreds of people." I said.

"Well it is the Army and I guess they have as many as they need. Has anyone given any kind of guess as to how long this thing is going to last?" Dad asks.

"Most everyone that I've talked to says it will take at least a year to get this all cleaned up. They said that a lot had to do with people. If they start going off and looting and rioting and destroying things then it could be a lot longer." The sheriff said.

"You know the people here in Perry; they aren't going to do that. We always help each other out and no one is going to start going off here." I said.

"It's not the folks around here that I'm worried about. It's the people that come here from out of town or even out of state. Especially since we are going to have this large F.E.M.A. camp here. People are already streaming in here." The sheriff said.

CHAPTER NINE

IT DOESN'T ADD UP

" I can't believe that after all this trouble it's a music CD." I said.

"Well it's Lindsey Stirling so at least it's a good music CD. Now you will have music to listen to." Molly said.

"True, my iPod still works but I had just erased it getting ready to put some new tunes on it so it's worthless except as a watch. I'll copy this CD over to it before we take the laptop back." I said.

"Why are you going to take it back, why don't you just keep it?" Molly asks.

"I don't want them coming after me thinking I have something that belongs to Shane." I said.

Molly starts going through the files on the laptop.

"Well there is nothing on here except a gazillion pictures of you. This boy has it bad for you." Molly says.

"Give me a break. We grew up together. We've been best friends forever and there is nothing wrong with a friend having pictures of their friend." I said.

"Even if the <u>guy</u> friend likes to take the pictures of the <u>girl</u> friend into Photoshop and do things like this."

Molly turns the laptop so that I can see it and there on the screen is a picture of me with a big red heart drawn around me and the text at the bottom saying **The Love of My Life**.

"Oh! My! God! He never once told me that he liked me that way." I said.

"Well he certainly seems to be crushing on you now." Molly says.

I take the iPod off of my wrist and hand it to Molly.

"Copy that CD and any other music you find over to this. Make sure you eject the CD when you get done and write Lindsey Stirling on it so we know which one it is. When we go over to get Biscuit we will take the laptop back." I said.

"The only computer on the planet that still works and you want to give it to the enemy." Molly said.

"You know you may be right. We might hang onto the laptop and see if they come to get it. If they do maybe they will tell us what's going on and where Shane really is." I said.

"Did I just hear a car outside?" Molly says.

I walk over to the window and look out. A man and woman get out of the car and walk to the front door.

"Who is it?" Molly asks.

"I'm not sure but they look really familiar. Let's go see." I said.

As Molly and I enter the front room, My mom is answering the front door. There is an older man and woman standing on the porch.

"Yes, may I help you?" Mom says.

The man sticks out his hand.

"Hi, I don't know if you remember us. I'm Malcolm Stevens, and this is Beverly. We are Joslyn's parents."

"Oh sure come on in." Mom says.

"We don't mean to disturb you. We were just wondering if you knew where Joslyn is." Malcolm says.

"No, actually we were wondering that ourselves. Have a seat." Mom says.

They all sit down on the couch. I can no longer contain myself and I blurt out.

"Where do you guys live?" I said

"Tulsa," Malcolm says.

"I knew it!" I said.

"Abby, just hold on." Mom says.

"What's going on?" Beverly says.

"Well Joslyn, Henry, and Shane are supposed to be staying with you," Mom says.

"At your home in Enid," I said.

"I'm sorry I don't understand." Beverly says.

"Well we've been trying to find out where they are? We went over to the house about a week ago and they were not there. Looked like no one had been there in a few days. Joslyn had not told me anything about going anywhere, and she always asks me to watch their house. So we drove down to the sheriff's office and asked the sheriff if he knew where they were. He didn't and said he would check it out. Then, yesterday he came by and said that he was told that Henry was volunteering to help in the relief efforts that Vance Air Base was holding and that he took the family up to stay at your home in Enid." Mom says.

"Who would have told him that?" Beverly asked.

"Our friends, the government." I said with air quotes around friends.

"We have this Colonel Krom here that has been coordinating the relief efforts here in Perry. He's on some task force set up by the president." Mom says.

"We haven't heard from Joslyn or any of them since we were here right before Christmas, and of course with phones and stuff being down we had no way to hear from them, so we decided to use the last tank of gas we had to come here and make sure they were all ok." Beverly says.

"Where could they be?" Malcolm asked.

"We don't know." Mom said.

"Someone told us that they thought they saw them out at the Warren ranch." I said.

"The Warren ranch?" Beverly asked.

"Yea, F.E.M.A. set up a communications facility out there and someone from the ranch said they thought they saw them being escorted into one of the buildings." I said.

"Well I guess we need to go out there and see what they are doing there." Beverly says.

"We went out there and it is a heavily guarded fortress and they won't tell you anything." Mom says.

"So what are we supposed to do?" Malcolm asked.

"I think we should go ask the colonel where they are since we have the evidence that he lied to the sheriff." I said.

"I don't think that's a good idea." Molly says.

"Why not? I ask.

"We might end up disappearing to." Molly says.

"Well then let's go see the sheriff and show him he was lied to by the colonel." I said.

"I think we should not go anywhere until your dad gets back." Mom says. "I want to see what he thinks about all of this."

"Well I think we need to go over to the house and get some rest. It took us over eight hours to get here and I'm really beat." Malcolm said.

"Why did it take so long to get here?" Mom asked.

"The roads are really backed up with stalled cars and people trying to get you to give them a ride or give them your gas." Malcolm says.

"It is really getting bad out there. That's one of the reasons we decided to risk coming here now. Before it gets any worse." Beverly said.

"Why don't you guys just crash here?" I said.

"That's ok we will go over there in case they should show up. Besides I think I need to take care of the animals. I'm sure they need some attention." Malcolm says.

"We were just over there and the feeders and everything seemed to be working ok." I said.

"There was a lot of poop in the stable." Molly said.

"We'll go over there and take care of everything." Malcolm says.

"When Jerry gets back I'll tell him about all this and see what he thinks we should do." Mom says.

Malcolm and Beverly get up and leave. As soon as they are out the door I start in.

"Now are you people going to listen to me? I've been telling y'all since day one that something was up with Shane and that the colonel was involved. But noooo. I was Nancy Drew and blah blah blah. Now you see I was right." I said.

"Well I have to admit that something weird is going on and it looks like the colonel should have the answers to what that is. Right now I'm more concerned with what the Steven's said about how long it took them to get here. It's only ninety-five miles and usually takes about an hour and a half. He said it took eight hours for them to get here. I can't believe it's that bad out there.

All those poor people with no way to get anywhere. They can't stay home they will starve to death and if they do try to get somewhere there is no fuel and there are other people that will take what food and fuel you have." Mom says.

There is a car door slam out in the front yard.

"That's probably your dad." Mom says.

I jump up and run to the door.

"It's dad." I said

I open the door and as he walks in mom gives him a big hug.

"Wow. What's up with that?" Dad says.

"I'm just glad to see you and glad to see you're ok." Mom says.

"I'm fine. I have some clothes for Molly in the car. Molly's parents said she could stay a couple more nights. But that's it." Dad says.

"We have an interesting bit of information." Mom says.

"O yea. What?" Dad asks.

"Well you know how the sheriff said that the Bevil's were staying with Joslyn's parents that lived in Enid?" Mom says.

"Yes." Dad says.

"Well they don't live in Enid they live in Tulsa like." I said.

"Ok, so he made a mistake about where they lived. No biggy." Dad says.

"Not only did he make a mistake about where they lived but he also made a mistake about the Bevil's staying with them." Mom says.

"And how do you know that?" Dad says.

"Well the Stevens, Joslyn's parents, just left here. They haven't seen Joslyn or any of them since before Christmas." Mom says.

"Really? That's crazy. Why would the colonel tell the sheriff that?" Dad asked.

"To stop him from snooping around looking for them." I said.

"The Stevens went back over to the Bevil's. They were worn out. It took them eight hours to get here from Tulsa." Mom said.

"Eight hours. Why so long?" Dad asked.

"They said there were people and cars all over roads trying to get rides and borrow gas." Mom said.

"Well I just talked to Pastor Gleason and he said that he is hearing that Las Angles and New York both look like a war zone. They are saying that there are bodies just lying out in the streets. A lot of buildings have been burned. It's really bad. But, he did say that they have the power back up in D.C. And think they will have it up in Oklahoma City tomorrow. That will help a lot. At least people will be able to see that eventually they will get this thing fixed." Dad says.

"People still won't be able to buy food." I said.

"True but they should be able to get the water going with power to the pumping station and gas pumps should start working again." Dad says.

"Sure, if you got cash to pay for the gas." I said.

"Well at least there making progress." Molly says.

"I also talked to that F.E.M.A. woman, Maria, while I was in town. She said they were going to open the camp on our place and start feeding people tomorrow. If y'all go riding or walking or whatever I don't want you going anywhere near that place. There is going to be a lot of strung out people going in there and I don't want you anywhere near them. Understand?" Dad says.

"Yes dad I understand." I said.

"Ok Jerry what are we going to do? We know the Bevil's aren't off on some relief mission. Joslyn's parents are worried sick about them, and so am I. We have to find out where they are." Mom says.

"I'll use the F.E.M.A radio to call the sheriff and see if he will come by in the morning. When he gets here we will go over to the Bevil's and talk to Joslyn's parents. I don't know anything else to do at this time." Dad says.

"Molly and I want to go with you when you go over there." I said.

"Sure you can go. I will need help cleaning all that poop out of the stables." Dad says.

"Well with any luck Mr. Steven's will have that done by the time we get there." I said.

Dad gets up and goes over to the F.E.M.A. Radio and calls the sheriff. I tell dad not to say anything about what he wants because I am sure the colonel and Maria will be listening in.

CHAPTER TEN

ONE SLIP

Morning came and dad did his usual yelling session to get everybody up and prepared for breakfast. I think the one thing that keeps us from realizing that the rest of the country is in such bad shape is the fact that we have plenty of food. Mom and Dad took food that we grew in the summertime and canned or froze it and stored it in the basement. We always lived through the winter on things we produced during the spring and summer. Dad would fatten up a steer and a pig each year and they would be put in the freezer. That was just the way it was with us and most of the farms in our area.

So as I came down to a great breakfast of pancakes and sausage it was just another day. We still had some power issues but like everything else dad kept enough butane, gasoline, and diesel to keep us going through a bad winter. After all these years of being prepared, the time finally came that we needed the stuff.

"Molly you need to redo the copying job you did on my iPod. One track sounds like ball bearings being fed into a sausage grinder." I said.

"You know what ball bearings being fed into a sausage grinder sounds like?" Molly asks.

"Please don't tell me you tried running ball bearings through my sausage grinder?" Dad said.

"No I'm just guessing that that's what it would sound like."

"Give me your iPod after breakfast and I'll plug it back into the laptop and try again." Molly said.

"You have a working laptop?" Erica asks.

"Oops." Molly said.

"Sort of." I said.

"Where did you get a laptop that works and why haven't you blown it up like you did mine?" Erica asks.

"We learned how not to blow it up by blowing up yours." I said.

"I'm still waiting for the answer to <u>where</u> you got a laptop?" Dad says.

"It's Shane's." I said.

"Shane's? How did you get Shane's laptop?" Dad asked.

"I borrowed it while we were over there." I said.

"You borrowed it?"

"Yes, Shane won't care."

"I'm not worried about Shane. If your story about him is true then it may have something on it that the government wants to see."

"It doesn't, I looked at all the files and there is nothing there except pictures of Abby, Biscuit, and Zea." Molly says.

"That's nice but the government doesn't know that, and I'm sure they would want to decide that for themselves."

"Then why didn't they take it when they took Shane's computer?" Molly asks.

"They took his computer?" Mom says.

"Yep."

"Why didn't you mention that when you came back from over there?" Dad asked.

"You said for me to quit acting like Nancy Drew, and to be honest, I figured you wouldn't listen anyway." I said.

"OK! What else did you notice when you were over there?" Dad asked.

"Nothing, just the computer and his clothes." I said.

"His clothes?"

"Yep." I said.

"All of them?"

"No, just his winter clothes." I said.

"Was Joslyn's clothes gone?" Mom asked.

"I don't know, we didn't look." I said.

"They probably took the clothes to make it look like they had left, and give credence to the whole helping out in Enid story." Dad says.

"Wow! You are starting to come around to the dark side." I said.

"You just make sure you take the laptop back when we go over there." Dad says.

"I was already planning on it." I said.

"Everyone eat." Mom says.

After breakfast we waited for the sheriff to get there and after dad had a short talk with him we loaded into mom's car and followed the sheriff over to the Bevil's farm. When we pulled up to the front of the house, Shane's grandfather was standing out front with Biscuit. As we got out of the car dad and the sheriff walked over and introduced themselves.

"Good morning Mr. Stevens, I'm Jerry Tate and this is our sheriff Brett Hardery."

"Just call me Malcolm. Glad to meet you although I think I've met you before Jerry."

"I think we have." Dad said.

"Why don't we all go inside and see if we can get Beverly to get some coffee or hot chocolate going?"

After tying Biscuit to the front porch railing we all went inside.

Mom, Dad, Malcolm, and the sheriff all set down at the kitchen table. Beverly put some water on the stove to heat up and Molly and I grabbed chairs from the den and moved them over to the kitchen table and sat down.

"Well sheriff do you have any ideal where my daughter and her family are?" Malcolm asked.

"No sir I don't. This Colonel Krom told me that they were with you, which was obviously wrong. Either he got things mixed up or he is deliberately trying to hide where they are and I don't think he is the type person to get things mixed up."

"So what do you think is going on?" Malcolm asked.

"I'm not sure. The problem is that with all our communications down it makes it very difficult to carry on an investigation."

"Sheriff, I had the foreman from the Warren ranch tell me that he saw the Bevil's being escorted into one of the buildings out there early one morning." Dad says.

"Really. Did he say whether they looked like they were being forced to go along or if they seemed to be agreeably going along?" The sheriff asked.

"He really didn't say, but he did say he was almost positive it was them."

"Ok. I guess I will go out there when I leave here. Mrs. Stevens have you found anything unusual or out of place here at the house?" The sheriff asked.

"No, not really. Looks like they took most of their winter clothes, but that's all. Oh and I did find this weird thing in the flowerpot on the cabinet while I was watering the plants."

She reaches into the pocket on her apron and pulls out a small electronic looking device. The sheriff stands up and waves to get everybody's attention then he puts his finger to his lips telling everyone to be quiet.

"That just looks like the receiver off of one of Shane's radio controlled cars. It probably landed there after one of his epic crashes." I said.

The sheriff gives me a big thumbs up and says.

"You're probably right. How's that coffee coming along the" The sheriff asked.

"I believe it's ready." Beverly says. "Is anyone hungry because I'm starving and I would be happy to fix something."

The sheriff makes a motion with his hands like he is writing on a piece of paper. Mom jumps up and goes into the den and grabs a tablet and pencil and hands it to him.

"How do you like your coffee Jerry?" Beverly asks.

The sheriff writes in big letters on the pad **They are listening to us** and shows it to everyone.

"Ok folks I wish I had more to tell you, but I'm sure everything is all right. I'll drive out to the Warren place and see if the colonel can explain what's going on. I'm sure he has a logical explanation for everything." The sheriff says.

"If we can be of any help or if you get any news please come by and let us know. Obviously we are going to stay here for now so we can look after the animals." Malcolm says.

The sheriff walks to the front door to leave and turns and once again puts his finger to his lips.

"I'll see you folks later."

Dad gets up and walks outside with him. I follow right along behind. When we get out to the sheriffs car he turns to dad and says.

"They obviously have the placed bugged. Be very careful what you say in there. I'm sure that's not the only one they placed in the house. I think we are dealing with something out of our league here. So be very careful. We probably already tipped our hand and they know we know, so once again be careful. I will come back to your house when I leave the ranch."

"Ok sheriff, we will be waiting." Dad says.

The sheriff gets in his car and leaves and dad and I walk back into the house. Molly is telling the story of how she met

Shane and appeared to be trying to act like everything was normal.

"Abby can you and Molly take Biscuit back to the barn? He's been standing there tied to the front porch all this time." Malcolm says.

"Make sure you put him in the barn and come straight back." Dad says.

Molly and I go out and untie Biscuit from the porch and walk him around to the barn. As we start to open the barn door Biscuit has a bad reaction and starts backing up.

"Settle down dork. We have to put you in there."

Biscuit refuses to go in the barn.

"What is wrong with you?"

Biscuit rears up and jerks the reins out of my hand and takes off running. I open the barn door and Molly and I walk in. The door quickly closes behind us and there are two guys standing there. One of them reaches for me and one reaches for Molly then everything goes black.

"How long can it take for them to walk to the barn and back?" Mom says.

Dad stands up and walks to the front door.

"Biscuit is standing out here by the porch. What are those girls up to now?"

Dad walks out on the front porch and Biscuit turns and starts prancing off.

"Whoa Biscuit. Take it easy." Dad says.

Biscuit runs around the corner of the house and then stops. When dad catches up to him he starts to run toward the barn.

"What are you doing," Dad yells as he starts to follow him?

When he gets to the barn biscuit is standing in front of the door pawing the ground and waiting for dad to get there. Dad opens the barn door and try's to walk in but Biscuit pushes him out of the way and goes in ahead of him.

"You crazy horse. What is wrong with you?"

Biscuit runs through the barn to the back door, which is standing wide open. There is no one there.

"Abby!!" Dad yells. "Where the heck are you?"

He grabs Biscuit's reins and tells him to calm down.

"There around here somewhere, just relax." Dad says.

Dad leads Biscuit into the barn as the Bevil's other horses start to come up. He shuts the back door and slides the bolt closed. Once again he yells for Abby and Molly with no response. Malcolm walks into the barn.

"What's going on?"

"I can't find the girls." Dad says.

"They probably walked out back to check on the other horses." Malcolm says.

"I looked back there and didn't see them and all the other horses are at the back door. Biscuit was acting really strange. Like something was wrong."

They both ran out of the barn and begin yelling. Mom and Beverly came out of the house to see what was going on.

"What's wrong?" Mom said.

"We can't find the girls." Dad said.

"I'm sure they're goofing off somewhere." Beverly says.

Malcolm yells from the backside of the barn.

"Ya'll come look at this."

They ran around to the backside of the barn and Malcolm was standing there pointing at the ground.

"There are fresh tire tracks here." Malcolm says.

"Oh my God Beverly cries out."

Mom starts yelling, "No, no, no. Jerry somebody took them, oh my God, someone has taken them."

Dad started walking and following the tire tracks. He followed them all the way to the back gate on the far side of the farm. He then came running back.

"We've got to go get the sheriff. Malcolm y'all stay here and watch for them in case they show up. We will go by the house and check on Erica and Harlan and see if they are ok. I'll try calling the sheriff on our radio at home and let him know what has happened." Dad says.

"He needs to watch and see if they show up out there at the communication center." Mom says.

"I can't believe this is happening." Beverly says.

"The sheriff and I will talk to the colonel because I know he is behind this. If the girls show back up here bring them to the house and call me on the radio."

CHAPTER ELEVEN

DENIAL

D ad pulls up to the front of the house. Mom jumps out of the car and runs into the house yelling for Erica and Harlan. They are setting on the floor playing a board game. Harlan jumps up and says, "What's the matter mom?"

"Thank God you're ok". She says.

"What's going on?" Erica asks.

"They have taken your sister." Mom said.

"What? Who took our sister, who took Abby?" Harlan yells.

Mom starts screaming and crying, "We don't know!"

"What the heck happened?" Erica asks.

"Her and Molly took Shane's horse back to the barn. We were all in the house and they decided to put the horse up. They walked him down to the barn. After about twenty minutes I went to look for them and they were gone." Dad said.

"Where did they go?" Harlan asks.

"We don't know. But they will be ok." Dad said.

Dad walks over to the radio and frantically starts trying to call the sheriff. The sheriff responds.

"This is sheriff Hardery, what's up Jerry?"

"Abby and Molly have disappeared." Dad Said. "We were at the Bevil's and they walked Shane's horse around to the barn and that's the last we saw of them." Dad says.

"How long ago was that?"

"About a half hour." Dad says.

"Where are you now?"

"We are at home. We came here to check on Erica and Harlan and use the radio to call you." Dad says.

"I'm headed that way. I'll have a couple deputies go to the Bevil's. Have you notified Molly's parents?"

"No not yet." Dad says.

"I'll send someone over to their place."

"Sheriff is the colonel out at the ranch?"

"No. I'm leaving there now and the guards say he hasn't been there all day."

"I know he is involved in this." Dad says. "I hope your listening colonel. You better get over here and start explaining what's going on and where my daughter's at."

"Hang on Jerry I'll be there in about fifteen minutes. Try to stay calm. You going ballistic is not going to help find your daughter." The sheriff said.

"All I'm saying is he better have some answers and if they harm Abby or Molly in any way he will have hell to pay. Did you get that colonel?" Dad said yelling into the microphone?

After about fifteen minutes of waiting the sheriff car pulls into the driveway with red lights flashing. The sheriff gets out of his car and dad walks out to meet him.

"Jerry I think we should go over to the Bevil's so I can have a look around. Why don't you, Angela, and the kids get into my car and we will drive over there."

Dad yells for them to come out and tells them what is going on. As they get in the car the Sheriffs radio comes on and its one of his deputies.

"Sheriff I'm over at the Bevil's farm and didn't you say that someone would be here?"

The sheriff looks at dad.

"They were supposed to stay there and wait. If the girls showed up they were to come straight here." Dad says.

"That's right, they should be there," The sheriff says.

"Well sheriff there is no one here. Did they have a car?" The deputy asks.

"Yes, a blue Fiesta. It was parked in front of the carport."

"Not here now and I've looked down at the barn and around and there is no one here." The deputy says.

"All right we will be there in five minutes."

"What the heck? Where do you think they went?" Mom asks.

The sheriff starts the car and they start to back up. All of a sudden four military Humvee's come pulling into the drive blocking the sheriff so they couldn't leave.

Soldiers start getting out of the vehicles and approaching the car, we hear a familiar voice.

"Excuse me, Sheriff Hardery!"

The sheriff rolls down his window and there stands Colonel Krom.

"Sheriff Hardery can I speak to you for a minute?" The colonel asks.

The colonel opens the sheriff's door and waits for him to step out. Another soldier opens the back door of the car and asks everyone to "please come with him". As everyone is getting out of the car the sheriff demands to know what is going on.

"Someone needs to tell me what is going on right now." The sheriff demands.

"Sheriff Hardery I'm taking this family into protective custody." The Colonel says.

"On whose authority?" The sheriff asks.

"By the authority of the President of the United States. Now if everyone would please get into the front vehicle we can move along." The Colonel says.

"I don't want to move along; I want to know what is going on! I want to know what you have done with my daughter." Dad says.

"Mr. Tate the faster you do what I ask and get in the vehicle the faster you will get answers to these questions." The Colonel says.

Everyone except the sheriff gets into the Humvee. All the windows are painted black and there is no way to see out.

"Sheriff I will discuss this with you later. But for now I need you to call off your deputies and go back to your office. You are to speak to no one about this and if you do you will be in a lot of trouble. I now have custody of the Tate family and you have no need to pursue this any farther. Do you understand?" The colonel asks.

"No, I don't understand the sheriff replies."

"Well I would suggest you act like you do and stay out of this. This is the big boy stuff; this is not some "Cletus missing some chickens" deal like you are used to. Interfering in this could have disastrous consequences both for you and the country. Now you tell me you are going to stay out of this or I'll load you into one of these vehicles and it will be a long time before you see daylight." The Colonel says.

"I understand Colonel Krom." The sheriff replies.

"Good." The Colonel turns to his men and says, "Let's pull out."

Erica is crying, mom is freaking out, Harlan thinks it's awesome that he is getting to ride in an Army Truck. Dad is trying to calm everyone down. Colonel Krom slides open a small portal in the partition that separates the front of the truck from the back.

"I'm sorry for the inconvenience folks but if you just keep calm we will be to our destination shortly." The Colonel says.

Then he slides the portal shut. Dad hits the portal with his fist.

"Where's my daughter dad screams?"

Mom grabs dad and pulls him onto the seat.

"I'm sure they are taking us to the same place they took Abby." Mom says.

"Erica, start the timer on your watch. I want to see how long it takes us to get there so I can figure how far away from the house we are." Dad says.

After an hour and fifteen minutes of bumping around they finally came to a stop. They set still for another fifteen minutes and then they started up again. This time they only moved forward about twenty yards and then they stopped again. After ten more minutes the colonel opened their door and told them to step out. Everyone got out of the Humvee, which appeared to have stopped in some kind of a walled in area that had very bright lights around its perimeter. If you looked up all you could see was light and if you looked around all you could see was dark murky figures.

"Please follow me." The colonel says.

Everyone was led to a door in the side of one of the walls. The colonel opened the door and led them in. After walking through three other guarded doors, everyone was led into a room that had four bunk beds, a couch, a small refrigerator, coffee pot, and a foosball table.

"Make yourself at home, there's drinks in the icebox, I'll be back shortly." The colonel says.

"Dad, do you have any ideal where we are?" Erica asks.

"I'm not sure. I think we were driven around in circles to confuse us into thinking we had gone a long way. I think we are still somewhere close to Perry." Dad says.

"Do you think we are at the Warren Ranch? Mom asks.

"No. I was listening as we drove along. To get to the entrance of the Warren ranch you have to cross the railroad tracks. I never felt or heard us cross any railroad tracks and it seemed like we were on nice paved road for the whole trip."

"I wonder if this is where Abby is." Harlan says.

"I hope so." Mom says. Then she pulled him on to her lap and hugged him.

"Maybe we will get some answers when the colonel gets back." Erica says.

Someone knocks on the door. A soldier steps in with a notepad and pen in her hand.

"Hi folks. I'm Sergeant McKinley. The colonel has assigned me to you and I'm here to make this as easy as I can. It's already after noon so could I get you something to eat?"

"What you got?" Harlan asks.

"Anything you want."

"How about you just get us some hamburgers or fried chicken or something like that." Mom says.

"Nothing for me." Dad says. "Since we were just kidnaped and we are being held against our will it kind of killed my appetite."

"Ok maybe later on you'll want something."

"Do you know when the colonel will be back?" Dad asked.

"No sir I don't."

"Do you know if my daughter is out here?" Dad asked.

"No sir I don't."

"Can you tell me where we are?" Dad asked.

"No sir I can't. My job is to try and make you comfortable. I will go and get you some food. Would you want me to bring some board games back?"

"That would be cool." Harlan says.

The sergeant then turns and leaves the room. As soon as she goes out the door you hear a distinctive clank as she bolts the door. Dad walks over to the door and tries to open it. Then he kicks it with his foot.

"I can't believe our own government is treating us this way. I served four years in the same Army that there in. They have no right to treat us this way," Dad says.

"I agree," Mom said. "However she was being very nice and she is just following her orders. We need to keep a cool head and go along with whatever it is they are doing because it's the only way we can find out where Abby is."

"Do you think they brought Shane's grandparents here?" Erica asks.

"Probably so." Mom says.

"You know there is one-thing that's bothering me." Dad says.

"From the time we left the Bevil's house to the time the sheriff got there was about fifteen minutes. I stood at the front door watching for the sheriff the whole time. I never saw anyone drive by the house. The only way to get to or from the Bevil's is by driving by our house. Their house is the last one on the road. It dead-ends at their house. Unless they came and went through the backside of the farm and that's all mud during this time of year. They would have had to have something like a Humvee to get out that way. Well the colonel seems to have a few of those. Right. So he had to have been the one that took them also. But why would he go to that much trouble? All he would have had to do was wait until we were gone and drive down the road."

"Maybe they went out the back way because the deputies were coming in the front way." Erica says.

"I never saw the deputies go by either and I know that there patrol car can't make it the back way."

"Maybe the deputies went by while you were talking on the radio." Mom says.

"It's possible I guess but it would have all had to happen in like two minutes."

"Erica will you play foosball with me?" Harlan asks.

"Sure she will." Mom said.

CHAPTER TWELVE

THE GOLDEN LOCKET

"Abby! Abby! Wake up! Please! Wake up!"

"Molly, why are you yelling at me?" I said.

"Wake up!" Molly says.

"Where are we?" I ask.

"I don't know. We're in some kind of small room."

"What happened?" I ask.

"I don't know. I remember going into the barn and then the next thing I remember is waking up here." Molly says.

I sit up and look around. All I see is two cots, a table, and four chairs. The room is very dimly lit.

"I have a feeling were about to find out what happened to Shane."

The door opens up and two females dressed in military uniforms walk in.

"Oh, good, glad to see you're awake. I'm Sergeant Lewis and this is Corporal Sanchez. Would you both sit down at the table please?"

Molly and I both move over to the table without saying anything.

"First I want to inform you that I'm here on behalf of Colonel Krom. You have been brought here for two reasons. First and foremost is for your protection. There are a lot of people out there that want to know how your friend Shane did what he did to bring the whole country to its knees. You two being his friends, and removing items such as his laptop from his house, they may think you have the information that they are looking for. Secondly the U.S. Government wants to know what you know and we brought you here to learn that information."

Molly starts to say something and I stop her.

"Don't say anything!" I said.

"You need to understand we are on the same team Abby. We just want any information you might have to help protect your country. The faster we get it the faster you can return to your parents."

"Can we have a lawyer?" I ask.

"A lawyer? This is way beyond lawyers Abby. You need to stop acting like you have something to hide and just tell us what was on the laptop?"

"We're not saying anything." I said.

"Ok then, I'm not here to pressure you. You can stay here as long as you like. Your parents can worry themselves sick over you as long as you like. So just make yourselves at home. If you go out this door the restrooms are on the right. On the left is my office and straight ahead goes out into an open area so you can get some sunshine. We will bring you some food at five. And just so you know we also brought in Shane's grandparents. They're in the room next door but they haven't woke up yet."

"Is Shane being kept here also?" I ask.

"I'm not going to answer any of your questions until you answer mine."

She then turned and walked out the door.

"Why won't you tell them?" Molly asks.

I put my finger up to my lips and say, "Don't say anything". "Let's go outside and see if we can tell where we are."

We walk outside. The open area is a small space probably eighty feet square. It is surrounded on all four sides by modular buildings. You can't see anything over the buildings. I walk around and look closely at the top of the walls.

"You see that window over there?" I point to the window.

"Turn so your back is towards the window."

"Have you lost your mind Molly asks?"

"No, I know that they probably have our room bugged and out here they can't hear us. There doesn't appear to be any cameras along the walls but there is one inside that window and since it's the only window, as long as we aren't facing it, they can't read our lips when we talk." I said.

"Where do you come up with this stuff Molly asks?"

"I watch a lot of spy movies."

I stand beside Molly with my back to the window as we speak.

"Why don't you just tell them we don't know anything?" Molly asks.

"Because something isn't right here. If what they are saying is true and they brought us here to protect us. Then why didn't they just pull up to the house and tell my parents that they were going to take us into protective custody. We are law-abiding people and once they explained it my father would have agreed and went with us. Why did they abduct us the way they did?"

"But if they know we don't know anything then they will just let us go." Molly says.

"I'm not so sure. I think the fact that we were illegally taken is a problem for them and we might just disappear. They will keep us around as long as they think we know something. But I'm sure they will try to separate us and get us to talk so make sure you don't say anything."

"How can I say something when I don't know anything?" Molly says.

"Another thing that is really bothering me is when this Sergeant Lewis was talking to us, she said that giving her this information would help your country. Not our country but your country. Don't you find that strange?"

"Not really." Molly says.

"How do we know who these people really are? They could be anybody. What if it's some group of terrorist trying to find out about the virus?"

"Really? Do you really believe that some terrorist group is putting on this elaborate hoax to find out where you put the laptop? Really?" Molly asks.

"You just don't get it do you?" I ask. "Think about it. Why would they take the Bevil's?"

"If! They took the Bevil's." Molly says.

"I think it's simple." I said.

"Ok Nancy Drew tell me what's up." Molly says.

"Well, let's say that Shane actually did cause the Internet outage with his Monarch Virus. Nothing like this has ever been done before. Somehow they traced it back to Shane. Maybe he even told his parents about it just like he told me. His dad freaks out and calls the authorities and the authorities decide he's telling the truth and arrest him. Since he's a minor they take his mom and dad to. Plus, they probably didn't tell them they were arresting him, they probably told him they needed to stash him somewhere to protect them. Just like they are telling us."

"Then why are they being so secretive about it, why don't they just say yes we have him in protective custody?" Molly asked.

"Because they don't want anyone to know that it was Shane that created the virus. Not to protect him, but to make sure no one gets a hold of the Virus or the person that created it. Why? Because of its power as a weapon against whomever the government wants to use it against." I said.

"Maybe they have him somewhere trying to figure out how to fix it." Molly says.

"Well that does make sense to, but either way, the point I'm trying to make is that they want the virus and they will do anything to get it. We just happen to be in the wrong place at wrong time and we need to be very careful what we say until we are sure who we are dealing with and that we are going to be safe. Until then we trust no one."

As we are standing there talking, two familiar faces come out the door into the open area. Its Malcolm and Beverly.

"Oh my God!" I scream and Molly and I run to them and start hugging them.

"We are so glad to see you." Molly says.

"We didn't know y'all were here." Beverly says. "How long have you been here?"

"They just brought us here today." I said.

"This is so crazy." Beverly says.

"They just walked into the house and said we are taking you into protective custody. Then they brought us here. We didn't even know we needed protecting." Malcolm says.

"We are just really confused about all of this. But at least it will be over soon."

"I hope so." Molly says.

"Why do you say that Malcolm?" I ask.

"Well they told us if we would give them the information they wanted they would let us go back to Tulsa. We told them all we knew. They mainly wanted to know what you had done with the laptop and I told them that you had hid it in your father's barn." Malcolm says.

"Why would you tell them that?" I ask.

"Wasn't that what you said when we were setting at the table at Josh's house?" Malcolm asks.

"No I never mentioned it."

"Well I gave them some wrong information then. I hope they don't go over to your place looking for it."

"So what is on that laptop that they want so badly?" Beverly asks.

"I don't know." I said.

"So you didn't get a chance to look at it?"

"Oh yea we looked at it." Molly says.

"Can we go back in where it's warm?" Beverly asks.

"They probably have the place bugged so we can't talk in there." I said.

"So where did you put the laptop?" Malcolm asks.

I ignore his question and say, "Yea lets go back in I'm cold out here to."

We walk back in and all four of us go into the room that Molly and I were originally left in. The corporal walks in behind us and asks what we would like eat.

"I'm a vegetarian so I would just like some plain pasta with cheese sauce." I said.

"I'll have the same." Molly says.

"Nothing for me." Malcolm says.

"Me neither." Beverly says.

"I'll be right back with your food." The corporal says.

"Could you get a message to the colonel and tell him I would like to see him?" I ask.

"I'll pass that along." The Corporal says.

"Why do you want to see the colonel?" Molly asked.

"If I'm going to tell anyone what we found on that laptop, it's going to be him." I said.

"So you did find something on the laptop?" Malcolm asks.

"There was a lot of stuff on it." I said.

"Like what?" Beverly asked.

"I'll tell you when we aren't in a bugged room." I said.

"I don't think this room is bugged." Malcolm says.

"Let's change the subject." I suggest.

"Ok." Malcolm says.

"I wonder what mom and dad are doing right now?" I said.

"I bet they are freaking out just like my parents are probably doing." Molly says.

"I'm sure the colonel told them that he had you in protective custody." Malcolm says.

"So I wonder where Zea is." I said.

Where who is?" Malcolm asks.

"Zea." "You know, Shane's dog." Beverly says.

"Oh yea, I bet she's with Shane." Malcolm says.

"No, she disappeared before Shane did." I said. "I bet she misses not playing with Bonzo."

"I bet she does." Beverly says.

"So do you still live out by the BOK Theater?" I asked.

"Yes we do, same old place." Beverly says.

"I remember when I was like four years old Shane's parents took us up to the BOK to see the Wiggles and we stayed at your house. It was awesome they have this huge duck pond in their back yard that has gold fish in it. I remember that was the first time I had even heard of a gold fish." I said.

"Yes I remember that. I don't think Shane had ever seen one either." Beverly said.

"We need to go back to our room and rest a bit. This has me just totally exhausted and my blood pressure is probably off the charts." Malcolm says.

"When they took us they didn't grab any of my medication. I hope we can get them to either let us go or send someone out to get it." Malcolm says.

"Yea, I think we need to rest up a little ourselves." I said.

Malcolm and Beverly get up and make a hasty exit then Beverly sticks her head back in the door and says, "We need to get together and figure out what it is that they want and tell them. I'm afraid they may drag this out and without his meds I don't know how long he will last."

"So we need to tell them." Molly says.

I point to the door and I get up and walk out. Molly follows me. We walk to the center of the open area and I turn with my back to the window.

"Turn so they can't see your face." I said.

"Listen, I know you are going to think I'm crazy but that's not Shane's grandparents."

"What?"

"That's not Shane's grandparents!"

"Ok you have lost it." Molly says.

"That's the same people that came to your house yesterday and talked with us and your parents. Your dad said he remembered them."

"People always say that when someone says <u>you may not remember me</u> even if they don't remember it. They think it would be impolite to not remember them."

"Whatever. Why do you think it's not them?"

"Ok, don't you think it is weird that they ask how long we have been here when they were there this morning when we were abducted?"

"Maybe they were just groggy from being rendered unconscious like we were." Molly says.

"Another interesting point you bring up. When this Sergeant was telling us they were here she said that they hadn't woken up yet. Implying that they were drugged just like we were."

"Ok, what's wrong with that?" Molly asks.

"Well when <u>they</u> were telling us about being taken, they said that they were at home and the people came in and told them that they were being put into protective custody, and then they were brought here."

"You're right." Molly says.

"Then Malcolm called Joslyn Josh. Joslyn hated being called Josh. I can't see her father calling her a name that she hated and no one ever called her. Another thing. They both said they weren't hungry. When we were at the house just hours ago Beverly said she was starving to death."

"So." Molly says.

"They had to take them right after they took us and during that time they were all outside looking for us."

"True but maybe she just lost her appetite." Molly says.

"Ok, how about this. Malcolm didn't even know who Zea was and I called Zea a "she" Beverly not only didn't correct me but she also turned around and call him a "she". Plus it was Malcolm that wanted us to take Biscuit to the barn where they were waiting to grab us. So noticing all of this and that some of it was kind of flimsy I decided to really test them so I made up the whole thing about them living near the BOK Theater in Tulsa. I have never been to the BOK Theater to see the Wiggles or anybody else and the whole duck pond thing was from my grandparent's house."

"Oh crap." Molly says. "Why do you think these people are doing this?"

"Because they want to know where the Laptop is and if there is anything on it that will help them get or crack the Monarch. Didn't you get suspicious when they kept asking us about it?" I ask. "So we can't trust them and I don't think any of these people are who they say they are. That's why I ask for colonel Krom. We know that he is with <u>our</u> government and if he shows up we will at least know we are still working with the right team."

I look down and see a little gold speck on the ground. I bend done at try's to move it with my finger but it won't move. I then start digging around it until I'm able to pry it out of the dirt.

"OH My God." I said.

Molly says, "What is it?"

"I know where we are."

"What?" Molly says.

"I know where we are. This is my locket. I lost it two years ago when mom, dad, Erica, Harlan, and I were riding horses out at the old Perry Airport. An Armadillo spooked Erica's horse and he lunged and hit my horse knocking me off. I lost the locket when I fell. When I noticed it was gone we came back and looked for it for an hour but could never find it. It was special because it was a gift from PamPa and I thought I would never see it again. What are the odds of finding it now?"

"So that means we are out at the old airport." Molly says.

"Yes it does. This has to be some of the mechanics shops that were by the old terminal building."

CHAPTER THIRTEEN

THE SMELL OF FEED CORN

It had been nearly six hours since the colonel said he would come back. It was dark outside and there was only one small light in the ceiling. Harlan had tired of playing foosball and he and Erica had lain down on their bunks.

"You know Angela; I think the colonel is staying away because he doesn't want to answer our questions." Dad says.

"The only questions I want answered right now are where Abby is and if she's ok. She has to be scared to death." Mom says.

"I'm sure she's ok but I don't think the colonel has her."

"What? Why would you say that?" Mom says.

"Because it doesn't make sense. Why would he keep us separated? Keeping us separated only causes more problems and a situation that the colonel doesn't want to deal with. I can't think of any reason that he wouldn't want us together and a lot of reasons he would." Dad says.

"Then who do you think has her?" Mom asks.

"I don't know."

Mom sets down on the side of the bunk and starts to cry. Dad walks over and sits down beside her and puts his arm around her.

"It will be all right. She is a very bright kid. So is Molly. If anybody can get through this they can." Dad says.

"My baby is out there somewhere and I don't know if she is cold, hungry, hurt, or even alive." Mom says.

The Colonel knocks on their door then opens it and walks in.

"I'm sorry I took so long he says. I got tied up trying to handle the crowed of people that has shown up at the F.E.M.A. camp out at your place. They fed five thousand out there yesterday and they have about three times that many out there now."

"I'm really not interested in all that. I want to know what you've done with my daughter." Dad asks.

"I don't have your daughter Mr. Tate. I wish I did have her and Molly but the truth is we don't know where they're at."

Mom starts to cry and tries to say something but can't.

"I'm sorry Mrs. Tate. I wish I could tell you where she is and who took her but I can't."

"This is insane! Why would someone take her? She didn't have anything to do with this virus thing." Dad says?

"No she didn't, but she does know Shane and Shane talked to her right after he released his virus. Add to that the fact that Mrs. Tate and her went over to his house looking for them and then shortly thereafter Molly and her went over to his house and if the rumors that correct she took his laptop. So they think she might have the info they want. She may have this information and not even know it. They can't get to Shane so there trying the only lead they have."

"They, you keep saying they. Who are they?" Dad asks.

"Well we know for a fact that there are at least three agents from China, One from Afghanistan, Six from Iran, and three from Russia in this area."

"Why don't you arrest them? Mom asks.

"We can't. They have done nothing that we can arrest them for. So far."

"Kidnapping my daughter is something." Mom says.

"We have no evidence to support that. The big problem is we have very limited communication with anybody so it's very difficult to track or even know where these people are."

Two soldiers come into the room and address the Colonel.

"Sir we are here about that task you wanted us to do."

"Right, Mr. Tate I need you to write down any thing you can think of that we need to take care of at your farm. These two men will be taking care of your farm for the next few days until we can figure out what we are going to do with you to keep you safe."

"Why can't they just escort me out there and I'll take care of it. Then I can return here?"

"We don't want these people to have a chance of finding out where you are. So we will do it this way for now. Ok. We had to take you out of there so quickly we didn't give you time to grab any clothes so if you would like for them to grab some while they're out there then just tell them what."

There is a knock at the door and another soldier steps in.

"Colonel I have the Tanton's out here."

"Please bring them in."

Molly's parents are brought into the room and are recognized immediately by the Tate's. Mom grabs Molly's mom and starts hugging her. The Colonel says, "I felt that since you were all out here and in the same predicament that you should be allowed to get together. I want you to understand that you're not prisoners out here. We are just doing this for your protection. I will also let you have limited access to our communications room so that you can hear some of the news from around the country. I think you need to understand how bad things are out there right now and what we have to deal with.

No one ever thought that something so simple, a few lines of code, a few commands, could change life all over the world. How did the world get so dependent on something so complex that no one can manage it let alone protect it? The world's ever increasing dependence on the Internet made it the target of every whack job on the planet. The more the government claimed it was safe, hack proof, and that there was absolutely the best way to make your business transactions, the more of a target it became.

So some twelve-year-old boy writes some code to try and get revenge on some kids that had done him wrong and here we are. All things digital are dead. He called it the "Monarch Virus" after the butterfly because his science teacher was obsessed with time travel and the butterfly effect. You know, a butterfly flaps his wings in the distant pass causes a hurricane now.

The Monarch virus, you would think that a virus that brought the world to its knees would have a more ominous name like the Final Revelation Virus or something.

Anyway you folks take some time and talk things over. If you need anything pick up that phone by the door and someone will take care of you."

"So, you have Shane?" Erica asks.

"Why would you say that?" The Colonel responds.

"Well you called it the Monarch Virus, and mentioned the reason that Shane used the virus. Stuff that you would of had to get from Shane or Abby and you swear you don't have Abby."

"I don't have Shane." The colonel says with a lot of emphases on the I.

"So do you know where he is?" Erica asks.

"I can't answer that but I will tell you that him and his family are ok and very well protected."

"Ok so what's the plan Colonel? How long are you going to keep us here?" Dad asks.

"Until I feel it's safe for you to be out there."

"How will you know when we are safe? I mean what has to happen, do the bad people have to leave the country or do your guys have to come up with an antivirus, what?" Dad asks.

"Well it's hard to say and I'm not sure I have an answer for that. I have a feeling things are going to get a lot worse out there before they get better. Even if we came up with an antivirus tomorrow it's going to take a long time to get things back up.

Places like Los Angeles are reporting up to two hundred deaths a day just from people trying to feed their kids. No one can stand to see their children starving and they find someone with food and they try to take it and someone ends up getting shot. They have had a lot of people burn their houses by starting a fire inside the house just trying and keep warm. There have been a lot of people in the northern states freeze to death and even in the Tulsa and Oklahoma City areas people are getting sick and dying from drinking contaminated water.

Of course the Stock Market is totally down so that stops the flow of money and will have devastating effects on a lot of businesses. And the list goes on and on. So even if they get the utilities back up it's still going to take a long time to get things functioning again. But we will.

It's somewhat ironic that some of these third world countries are doing great. They never had computers or networks and nothing has changed for them. To them its business as usual. Anyway make sure you get that information to us and we will try to help you take care of your farm while you're here."

The Colonel gets up and leaves and mom asks Molly's parents, Tina and Tim, to sit down.

"So where do you think they are?" Tina asks.

"I don't know. I'm pretty sure that they aren't here at the ranch and I really don't think the Colonel has them or knows where they are." Mom says.

"I'm so scared." Tina says.

"There is no way to explain how I feel. They are so young. Molly has never been away from home and really she's never been away from us except for an occasional sleep over at your place." Tina says.

"I know, Abby is the same way." Mom says.

"So there were no tire tracks or anything around the barn?" Tim asks dad.

"Just one set and it led out the gate but we could tell nothing about it because the ground is still frozen, but there wasn't any trace of them and they weren't gone fifteen minutes before I started looking for them." Dad said.

"It was obviously professionals." Tim says. "We knew nothing about all this. We were getting ready to hay the cows when these four army vehicles come blaring into the driveway and the soldiers jumped out and came running at us."

"It scared the crap out of me." Tina said.

"When they got to us they were nice but very demanding telling us that we had to come with them. I ask what it was about and they told us we were being taken into protective custody. I screamed why and they just shoved me into one of their vehicles. Then they brought us here. Wherever that is." Tim says.

"We are at the Warren Ranch." Dad says. "The Colonel set up these buildings out here as a communication center. We came out here a couple days ago and the colonel was out here. He has never confirmed that is where we are but I'm sure it is. The smell of our feed corn and the quarter horses is unmistakable."

Three is a knock at the door and a soldier asks permission to come in. Dad says, "Yes come on in."

"Hi, I'm Private Penson, if you need to take a shower just let me know and I will bring you your toiletries and towels."

"Oh My God!" Erica says.

"Debra? Is it really you?" Erica says.

"Erica? I never realized that it was you and your family that we were holding here."

"You remember Debra don't you?" Erica asks everyone.

"Oh yea, you were one of the student teachers at the school a couple a years ago." Mom says.

"That was me." She says.

"How did you end up in the army?" Erica asks.

"After 911 I felt like I needed to do something to better serve my country so I joined up. Wow this is weird. I never expected to see anybody in here that I knew and you guys are the third ones to show up that I know."

"Who was the other one?" Dad asks.

"Oh, Shane and his parents are here, well his parents are here Shane took of two nights ago."

"Took off?" Dad asks.

"I'm sorry I shouldn't be telling you this stuff. Everything around here is so hush hush. I will get into big trouble."

"Our lips are sealed." Dad says.

"Thanks, I have to get back to my post. If you need anything let me know." She turns and leaves.

"The Bevil's are here." Dad says.

"Yea and Shane took off." Tim says.

"I wonder why we are able to talk to y'all but they want let us talk to them?" Mom says.

"Why don't we find out?" Tim says.

"Well, we have to do it in a way that doesn't let them know that the private told us they were here." Dad says.

"We don't want to get her in trouble and if she trusts us she might help us out by letting us know what's going on."

CHAPTER FOURTEEN

OLD FRIENDS AND FOES

A knock on the door brings both Molly and I out of a deep sleep. I jump up off my bunk and say, "OH my God, we must have dozed off. How long have we been asleep?"

"My watch says its 7:30 am." Molly says.

"Wow. We slept all night."

Once again there is a knock at the door. I stager over to it and open it. It's Beverly.

"Can I come in?" Beverly asks.

"Sure."

"I'm sorry to bother you this early in the morning but I want to ask, no beg, you to tell them what they need to know. Malcolm is very ill because he doesn't have his medication. They said we could go home if we would just tell them. The problem is we don't know anything."

"Well we don't know anything either." I said.

"Then you need to convince them of that. You have to know where the laptop is, give them that information and maybe they will let us go."

"I don't know where the laptop is. The last time I saw it, it was in my backpack setting next to the kitchen table at your daughter's house."

"Really?" Beverly asks.

"I'm sure they probably went through there very thoroughly so if they didn't find it someone else got to it before they did." I said.

"That's impossible. They came to the house minutes after you disappeared; no one would have had a chance." Beverly says.

"They would have had the chance." I said. "You said they came in and took y'all out immediately. So someone could have came in after you left. Right?"

"I guess so." Beverly says.

"I'm going to go tell them about this and maybe they will let us go." Beverly says.

I look at Molly and shake my head.

"We have to get out of here." Molly says.

"I'm going to the restroom." I said.

As I walk out and toward the restroom I see a reflection in the glass of one of the doors that leads to where the guards always go when they leave our room. In the reflection I see Malcolm and Beverly sitting at a table talking to Sergeant Lewis. Malcolm has his hands back over his head and appears to laughing. Beverly is shaking her head and laughing. I walk quickly by and into the restroom. I then return to our room and tell Molly to come outside. We assumed the position with our backs to the window.

"Those scumbags." I said.

"Who?" Molly asks.

"The Stevens. I just saw them talking and laughing with the guards. Didn't look like he was near stroking out because of the lack of medication. I also saw something else. Beside the guard, on a small table, was some radio gear, the same radio that F.E.M.A. was giving out. I'm sure they are using it to listen to the colonel or whoever as they talk on it."

"So, I would expect something like that wouldn't you?" Molly asks.

"Yes, but I didn't realize it would be within our reach. If we can catch them out of that room, one of us can run in there and try to contact my dad or the sheriff."

"How are we going to pull that off?" Molly asks.

"I don't know. They have to go to the restroom sometime. We have only seen the two guards and that corporal stays gone most of the time."

"What about the scumbags?" Molly asks.

"We will just lock them in their room. We need to learn more about what the guards do and where they go. Let's go back in."

As we enter the room the Sergeant follows us in.

"We'll have you ladies had time to think about what you know?"

"As I told you yesterday I will tell Colonel Krom what I know when he gets here." I said.

"The Colonel said it will be awhile before he can come by here, maybe even a couple of days, and that you need to tell me what you know." The Sergeant says.

"No. I will tell him and only him." I said.

"Why are you making this so difficult? The Steven's told us what they knew and we will be taking them back to Tulsa as soon as transportation is available."

"They didn't know anything so how did they tell you anything?" I ask.

"They knew what you did with the laptop."

"So, there is nothing on the laptop." I said.

"How can you be so sure if you didn't go through every file? One of our top computer guys can find stuff on there even if it's been erased. So where is it?"

"I thought the Steven's told you what I did with it." I replied.

"They told us the story that you made up about leaving it in your backpack under the table."

"That's what I did with it. Why would I make up a story like that for them? They are almost like grandparents to me."

"So what do you have to say Molly? Did Abby leave the laptop under the table?"

"I'm pretty sure."

"What do you mean <u>pretty</u> sure?"

"Well she walked into the house with it but I'm not sure where she set it down."

"Right! You two have this all figured out don't you? What I don't understand is why you guys want to do this to the people that are trying to help you. Do you think that we want to sit out here and babysit you to girls when this whole country is in a state of emergency? We could be out there helping feed some of those people that have lost everything because of this little stunt that your friend pulled. But no, we are here trying to extract information out of you. Did you know that if you were old enough you could be tried for treason for withholding this information from your government and interfering with a federal investigation?"

"Did you know that you <u>will</u> be tried for kidnapping minors and holding them against their will without their parents even being informed or without producing any kind of warrant or legal document showing that you have the authority to do such a thing?" I ask.

"Wow. You are as smart as they say you are, and that may be true, but at least I won't spend my time in prison thinking about all those people that starved to death because I didn't try to help." The Sergeant says.

"Then you need to get the Colonel out here so we can tell him what we don't know." I said.

"Ok. You can just set here until he shows up. May be days, and oh yes I forgot to tell you that do to the lack of power we will be shutting of the heat on this side of the building. I hope you girls don't mind the cold."

"Wow, now we can add torture to that list of charges." I said.

"I don't handle the cold very well Abby." Molly Says.

"Let's go back outside." I said.

We get up and walk out. As we pass the room that the Stevens were staying in we notice the door is partially open. I walk over to the door and knock on it while pushing it open.

"Is anyone here?" I ask.

No one replies so they go on in. The room is cleaned out like no one had ever been there.

"Wow I can't believe they really did release them." Molly says.

Once again I hold a finger up to my lips to indicate to Molly that they were probably listening to us. We look around for a minute and then proceed to go out into the open area.

"I guess they figured out that we weren't going to open up to the Steven's so they removed them." I said.

"That's what I figured to, that's why I said what I said. To make them think I thought they were released." Molly says.

"That's great. We are going to have to convince them that we aren't on to what they are doing and that we <u>might</u> give them some information. At least until we can get a chance to use that radio." I said.

"I saw where you said the radio was. It is directly across from the restrooms. If we could get the guard to come into our room then you could dismiss yourself to the restroom and then run in and make the call on the radio." Molly says.

"Wow, you're getting pretty good at this." I said.

"Well I have spent most of my life hanging around you." Molly says.

"I've noticed that the corporal spends most of her time in the far end building where the window is. I think she can see through our hall door and will probably be able to see me when I go into use the radio. If we can somehow kill the light in the hallway then she wouldn't be able to see me."

"The breaker panel is right outside our door." Molly says.

"The what?" I ask.

"The breaker panel that controls the electricity. If they have the breakers labeled, and this being the old airport, I'm sure they do, then we flip the breaker for the hallway lights, and no more lights."

"You gooood!" I said.

"How do you know that?" I ask.

"My dad is an electrician remember. I used to hang out at his shop and go on jobs with him. He taught me all about the biz."

"Cool." I said.

"If we get caught turning the power off then we tell them that we were trying to turn the heat back on and we got the wrong breaker." Molly says.

"Dang girl, I don't know if I should be scared or proud." I said.

"So when we go back in we flip the breaker it won't be noticeable until right after dark. So as soon as it starts getting dark you can call the guard in and tell her you want to talk. When she gets there I will tell her I'm going to the restroom and walk out. I will run to the radio and try to get someone to answer. Then I'll come back in the room." I said.

"Now we need to make up some story to tell her that's believable and long enough to give you time to do what you need to do. I'll tell her they were two executable files that were fairly large and they were encrypted. One was named start and one was named stop. And there also was some cracking and hacking tools like Wire Shark or something." Molly says.

"Ok the only real problem I see is if the Corporal also has a radio on her end of the building. I should be able to broadcast where we are before she would have time to get there and stop me. Well let's go back in and wait for dark."

As we walk back into the building Molly walks over to an electrical panel mounted on the wall next to their door. I stand in front of her so that anyone looking through the door wouldn't be able to see what she was doing. She opens it up and scans down the list of breakers until she finds one labeled

Hallway Lights. She flips the breaker to the off position and then quickly shuts the panel door.

"Done!" Molly says. So we walk into our room.

"What time is it?" I ask.

"It's 6:35." Molly replies.

"What happened to your iPod watch?" Molly asked.

"It's fine; I just have it turned off in case we need it because I don't have any way to recharge it." I said. "Well it should be dark in about an hour so let's enjoy the light while we can. Do you want to play go fish?"

"Sure why not?"

We played cards for about forty-five minutes.

"Well its getting dark." I said.

"Another day wasted setting in this stupid room." Molly says.

"You would think that they could see that we really don't know anything and let us out of this place." I said.

"I think I'm going to tell the Sergeant about the encrypted files I saw on the laptop." Molly says.

"Why would you want to do that? I told you unless we tell the Colonel we don't know who were giving the information to." I said.

"I don't care I can't take this any longer."

Their door opens up and in walks the Sergeant.

"So are you ladies enjoying your nice cool room? I also see that there are some lights out. I'll have that fixed in a week or two."

"I want to talk to you." Molly says.

"Please don't Molly." I said.

The Sergeant immediately sets down at the table.

"What do you want to tell me Molly?" The Sergeant asks.

"It's about the laptop."

"I don't believe this. I'm going to the bathroom." I said.

I get up and start walking out.

"Some friend you are" I sneer at Molly.

I walk out of the room. I freeze in my tracks when I see the corporal walking down the hall toward the door. As soon as the corporal is out the door I start walking toward the restrooms. When I get in front of them I turn and run into the office where the radio is sitting. Luckily it was turned on and operating. I pick up the microphone and very quietly begin to speak.

"Sheriff Hardery can you hear me?"

No response.

Again.

"Sheriff Hardery can you hear me?"

Then a voice comes over the radio speaker.

"Is someone out there calling for Sheriff Hardery?"

"Yes, I reply is this the sheriff?"

"Negative on that, this is deputy Murphy the sheriff is in the restroom. Can I help you?"

"Please, this is Abby Tate. We are being held in the old maintenance building at the old Perry Airport. I repeat this is Abby Tate and we are being held by terrorist in the old maintenance building at the old Perry Airport. Please help us." I plead.

"Is this some kind of prank?" The deputy asks. "Because if it is you're going to get in a lot of trouble."

"Please tell the sheriff or my father or if there is anyone listening to this on the radio please help us. Do not call me back or respond to me on the radio I repeat do not call me back or respond to me on this radio. They will be listening."

Then there is nothing but cross talk as more than one-person try's to talk at the same time. I reach down and turn the radio volume down and run out of the room. I walk back into the room where Molly is spinning a yarn about encrypted files and the Sergeant is buying every word of it.

"So are you through spilling your guts Molly?" I ask. The Sergeant gets up and tells Molly that she appreciates her help and that as a reward she would turn the heat back on. Then she leaves the room. I shake my head in an affirmative manner when Molly gives me a <u>did you do it</u> look on her face. Molly lets out a little squeal.

CHAPTER FIFTEEN

I'LL DO ANYTHING I CAN

Molly and I are setting at the table waiting.
"What should we do?" Molly asked.

"Just sit here and wait. How long has it been?"

"About thirty minutes."

The lights, and what appears to be all the power, suddenly go out. Molly starts to scream but muffles it.

"What the heck is going on?"

"I don't know, they probably ran out of gas in the generators." I said.

They set there in dead silence for about thirty minutes.

"Something isn't right, it's too quiet. Let's check it out." I say.

We get up and feel our way to the door and then go out into the hall. The moon shinning in through the window is the only light in the whole place. We walk down to the office to see the Sergeant. There is no one there and the radios appear to be gone.

"Let's go out into the open space and see if they are on the other side." I said.

We walk out and over to the far end door. There appears to be no power there either. We walk over and try to see into the window but everything is pitch black.

"Let's see if we can find our way out of here before they get the lights back on." I said.

"I don't think there is anyone here to turn the lights back on." Molly says.

We see the beam of a flashlight moving inside the hallway behind the door. We both freeze in place. The light comes through the door and we prepare to run. The light flashes across us and then comes back to us. We start running toward the other end of the open space. Then a loud voice rang out.

"Stop! Abby is that you?"

I didn't know where to stop or keep on running but the voice sounded familiar. I stop and Molly runs into me and we both fall down.

"Abby, Molly is that you?"

"Sheriff Hardery is that you?" Molly yells out.

"Yes it is." The sheriff yells back as he approaches us lying on the ground.

He shines the light toward his own face so that we could see that it was him. We both jump up and start jumping up and down and hugging him. Sheriff Hardery yells out, "I found them! We're in here!"

Two more flashlights come through the door as the sheriff's two deputies come running in.

"Are you girls all right?" The sheriff asks.

"We are now," I try to say but I break into tears. "We are now."

"Where is everybody?" The sheriff asks.

"I don't know. The power went off a while ago and we waited a while then came out and no one was here." I said.

"They must have taken off when they found out that Abby had used the radio." Molly says.

The sheriff tells the two deputies to continue looking around. "I'm going to take the girls and leave. I want to get them out of here before someone else shows up and tries to take them. Make sure you don't mention them on the radio. Wait about thirty minutes and call me on the radio and say what I told you to say."

"I'll call you and say that we have searched everywhere out here and could find nothing." The deputy says.

"Right, if you do find something just say, we are going to turn in for the night and then come to the office."

"Ok."

We walked out to the sheriff's car and he put us in the back seat. The sheriff gets in the front and we take off.

"Are you sure you're ok?" The sheriff asked.

"We're fine." I said.

"Have you had anything to eat or drink?"

"Yes we had a little to eat. I hadn't really been very hungry." Molly says.

"Do you have any ideal who was holding you out here?"

"They said they were with Colonel Krom but I don't think they were." I said.

"Why?"

"They were too disorganized to have been any kind of military trained personnel. We kept asking to speak to the Colonel and they never would get him." I said.

"Then the Steven's were obviously fake." Molly says.

"What do you mean?"

"They aren't really Shane's grandparents." I said.

"Really? You know I thought something was up there. I met Joslyn's parents like fifteen years ago when the Bevil's first bought that farm. I remembered both of them as being a lot shorter. When they just disappeared from the farm before we could get back there I felt something was not quite right.

I would be willing to bet that these people have nothing to do with the Colonel. Well anyway we will get full statements from both of you."

"Can you take us home?" I said.

"I'm not sure we want to do that." The sheriff says.

"Why not?"

"Well Colonel Krom took your parents into protective custody so there is no one at either of your homes and I'm sure your homes are being watched."

"By whom?" Molly asks?

"By everyone that wants to find out about that virus."

"Where are our parents?" I ask.

"We are pretty sure that they are out at the Warren Ranch. They took them so fast that I didn't have time to set up someone to follow them, but my source out at the ranch said they unloaded four people out there at about the same time that they took your parents."

"My parents are probably worried sick and scared to death." Molly says.

"I'm sure they are being treated well. They are in the care of the Colonel."

"I don't trust the Colonel either." I said.

"That's why I wanted to get you out of there as fast as I could. I'm sure the Colonel and a lot of people heard your radio broadcast and I really don't trust him either."

"Where are you going to take us?" Molly asks.

"I'm not sure yet. I'm going to drive around for a bit and see if anyone is following us. I think I'll take you to my house first. Donna can cook you a nice meal and you can clean up and put on some fresh clothes. In the mean time I will try to figure out where we can put you."

"Why can't we just go out to the Warren Ranch and stay with our parents?" I ask.

"That might be a possibility, but we need to make sure your parents are out there and that everything is ok out there.

I heard a rumor from a fairly reliable source that they had taken Shane up to the air base in Enid to better protect him and his family."

"I don't think they are really interested in his safety as much as they are the information that he has. That, and to keep someone else from getting to him and getting the information before they do." I said.

The radio lights up and Deputy Gleason voice comes blaring trough the speaker.

"Sheriff you copy?"

"Roger that." The sheriff says.

"Yea, sheriff we have searched everywhere out here and could find nothing."

"Roger that, why don't you guys just go ahead and head to the house. We will pick this up tomorrow."

"Roger that, do be advised that there were at least two other vehicles that showed up out here and they appeared to be military."

"Roger that." The sheriff says.

"Out."

"Well as I expected there were others listening to your radio broadcast. Luckily we know the area and were able to get to you first. I really hope I'm doing the right thing by not taking you to the Colonel. Although he has never instructed me to do that if I happen to find you."

"I really don't trust him but if it would allow us to get to our parents I would go out there right now." I said.

"I agree the sheriff says but the problem is we are not one hundred percent sure your parents are out there so if I take you out there and he decides to keep you isolated from them then you could both be there and not even know it. We have to come up with a way to deliver you with your parents standing right there so you can go to them. Even if he separates you afterward at least your parents would know you're ok."

"I just want to go home." Molly says.

"I understand." The sheriff says.

We pull into the sheriff's driveway and Donna, the sheriff's wife comes out on the front porch to meet us. The sheriff says for us to go straight into the house before someone spots us. As we enter the door the smell of food is permeating through the house and you could almost taste it.

"Girls, this is my wife Donna, although I'm pretty sure you have met before." The sheriff says.

"Oh yes, I've known them since they were babies." Donna says.

"Something smells really good." Molly says.

"Well the sheriff said that you were both vegetarians so I was able to put together a few vegetables, which happen to be my favorites to. Unfortunately things are starting to get pretty scarce around here so we are very limited on variety. Now you guys sit down and make yourself at home.

Brett, I went over to the church tonight to help them feed the people that come there for help and I ran into someone we haven't seen in years." Donna says.

"Oh yea who was that?"

"Your niece."

"Which one?"

"Debra."

"I thought she had joined the military and was in Afghanistan or Iraq or somewhere." The sheriff says.

"Well she was, but she had come home for Christmas and with all that has happened they canceled her leave and she got orders to stay here. Now she's stationed out at the Warren Ranch and reports to Colonel Krom." Donna says.

"Really! That's very interesting. Is she staying at her parents place?"

"Yes she is and she said she would love to see you."

"This maybe the break we have been looking for the sheriff says. She has to know who is out there."

"Yea, I'm sure she does, as a matter of fact I ask her if she knew and she said she couldn't tell me." Donna says.

"Well I bet she could deliver a message to the Tate's and Tanton's telling them that their daughters are ok. Even if she won't verify that they're out there she could still do that." The sheriff says.

"Are you talking about Debra Penson?" Molly asks.

"Yes she is Brett's niece." Donna says.

"I remember her." I said.

"She used to be our substitute teacher when Mrs. Grisham was out having her baby."

"That would be her." The sheriff says.

"I will go by there tomorrow and see her."

"You girls would probably like to clean up a bit. I don't know if we can find any clothes that will fit you but while one of you takes a bath I'll wash your clothes and stick them in the dryer and it won't take but a minute." Donna says.

"I can't think of anything better right now than a good hot shower." Molly says.

"Ok then you go first."

While Molly takes a bath the sheriff sets down to talk to me.

"Abby I want you to know that I'll do anything I can to help you and your parents."

"I know that." I said.

"But you have to understand that I'm just a small town sheriff and the Colonel with his Presidential authority can pretty much do whatever he wants to. If he shows up here and demands that I turn you over to him then I will have to do it."

"I understand." I said.

"I just brought you here to give us a little time to try and sort things out and figure out what to do. None of us around here has ever dealt with anything like this. Not just the crisis that is going on but also the whole thing about one of our kids being hunted by every country and every nut job in the world. There is no playbook on something like this and I'm just making it up as I go. So please believe me when I say I'm here to help."

"I do." I said.

"Is there anything you know that will help the Colonel find what he's looking for?"

"No, I don't know anything. We looked at Shane's laptop and there was nothing on it but pictures and music." I said.

"But you aren't computer savvy enough to be able to know if there was something hidden on it right?" The sheriff says.

"No, I'm not but Molly is. She is freakishly computer capable just like Shane." I said.

"And she looked at it to, right?"

"Yes she did."

"So where is the laptop?"

"I left it by the kitchen table in Shane's house."

"So we can assume that someone else has found it by now. I'll go by there in the morning and have a look around. In the mean time you guys get some rest and we will start trying to get you to your parents in the morning."

CHAPTER SIXTEEN

PUTTING THE PIECES TOGETHER

Being woken from a deep sleep by a lot of noise is not the way I like to wake up. I guess the sheriff and his wife never thought about how loud their alarm clock really was seeing how they have no kids or anybody else in the house to complain. Either that or they are both hard of hearing.

After a moment of silence I could hear the sheriff telling Donna that he was leaving to go to his niece's house before she went into work, and then I heard the door slam and it was all nice and quiet again.

"Molly you awake?" I ask.

"Who could sleep through that?" Molly replies.

"Man, when I got into bed last night I cranked up my iPod and was listening to Lindsey Stirling and I was just going to sleep when it hit that bad track and I almost jumped out of bed.

Then I couldn't go back to sleep so I just lay there all night trying to figure how we can get to our parents. I guess I finally went to sleep around 3:00 A.M."

"I went to sleep as soon as my head hit the pillow." Molly says.

"I think we should go ahead and get up." I said. "Let's go into the kitchen and see if Donna has any news."

We walk into the kitchen and Donna is already busy putting together some breakfast.

"I'm sorry girls." Donna says. "I should have turned the alarm down last night. It used to turn on the radio and woke you up with music but since there are no radio stations broadcasting it wakes us up with that god awful shrieking noise."

"That's ok." I replied.

"Have you heard anything new?" Molly asks.

"Nothing. The radio has been quiet. The sheriff, as you probably know, left early this morning to try and find out what he could. He said for y'all to just stay here until he gets back. I don't take you guys to be coffee drinkers so I can offer you Kool Aid or milk your choice."

"Milk." I replied

"Milk." Molly replied.

A car door slams outside and Donna walks over to the door to see who is out there.

"It's Murphy." Donna says.

She opens the door and tells him to come on in.

"Would you like coffee, milk or Kool Aide?" She asks.

"Little early for Kool Aid so I guess I'll have some coffee." Murphy replies.

"So how are you young ladies doing this morning?"

"We are doing fine." I replied.

"Where's the sheriff?" Murphy asks.

"He had a couple things he needed to do first thing so he has already left. He should be back shortly." Donna replies.

"Well I didn't call him on the radio, because he wants us to continue to stay off the radio, but I found something of interest last night out at the airport."

He reaches into his pocket and pulls out a small tablet. He hands it to me and I ask what it is.

"It appears to be a personal notepad of some type. If you look at the scribbling in it, it appears to be written in Chinese."

"Wow your right."

I hand it to Molly.

"So it was the Chinese that were holding us out there?" I ask.

"It appears so. It looks like this was dropped as they were making their hasty getaway. We can't know for sure but if we could get that stuff translated it might give us some useful information."

"How you going to do that?" Molly asks.

"How about Ricky Yeah, the guy that owns the hardware store? He might be able to read it." I said.

"That's true. I never thought of him. He has his store closed like everybody else but I know where he lives. I'll head over there right now." Murphy says.

"Shouldn't you wait a little while; it is six in the morning?" Donna says.

"I'll wait until the sheriff gets back. Make sure he's ok with it." Murphy says.

"If you guys are hungry I can whip up some breakfast?" Donna says.

"Sounds good to me." Molly says.

"Me to." I said.

"Me to." Deputy Murphy says.

After about an hour the sheriff gets back home.

"Well I didn't expect to see you here Murphy." The sheriff says.

"I found something that I thought you might be interested in."

"Oh yea what's that?"

He hands the sheriff the notepad.

"What's this?" The sheriff asks.

"It's a notepad that I found out at the airport. Looks like it got dropped when they were leaving."

"Is that Chinese?"

"I believe it is. Abby suggested that I get Ricky Yeah to translate what it says."

"That's a good ideal. Take it over there but make sure you don't tell him anything about where it came from or how you got it."

"Will do. I'll let you know what he says."

The deputy leaves and the sheriff gets a cup of coffee.

"Well I talked to my niece. She couldn't tell me much but she did confirm that both of your parents are out there. She said they were being well taken care of and are very stressed out about you to. She is going to try and pass the word to them that you guys are both ok. She also said that the Bevil's are out there but Shane had given them the slip and she's not sure where he is. One thing she did say is that if we take you guys out there they will keep you separated from your parents."

"Why would they do that?" I ask.

"Because of what happened with Shane. He was allowing them to stay together and due to that Shane was able to give them the slip. She didn't know exactly what happened but the colonel thinks it was because they were too lax on security. Debra made me swear that you three were the only ones I told this to, so make sure you don't say anything about it to anyone."

"Well it's not like we are going to be talking to anyone anytime soon." I said.

"I also went by the Bevil's place to look for the laptop. Someone had already been there looking for it and had pretty well trashed the place. Of course the laptop was nowhere to be found."

"Well if we can't join our parents, and they find out that we are ok, then there is no reason for us to go out there." I said.

"Only that there is a lot of very unsavory people out here that would love to get their hands on you." Donna says.

"So what are we going to do?" Molly asks.

"We are going to find Shane." I said.

"Personally, I think you should just stay here until it's safe for you to be out there. As far as I can tell nobody knows your here, so I think your safe." The sheriff says.

"What about going out to my house?" I ask.

"It's definitely not safe out there." The sheriff says.

"I don't mean to stay, I mean to pick up some clothes and stuff that we need." I said.

"I don't know about that, if they see you go in then they would either try to take you then, or watch and see where you go, so they can grab you later."

"Maybe if we waited until late tonight we could drive out there." Donna says.

"Why don't you just tell me what you need and where it is and I can get it."

"No that's ok; I really don't want someone digging around in my dresser drawers or my bedroom." I said.

"What about letting Donna go in and get your stuff. She knows what you need and what to look for."

"I guess we could do that." I said.

"Well I think, since no one knows where you are, they will be watching your house very closely to see if you show up there the sheriff says."

"What about my house?" Molly asks.

"To be honest with you they probably are not likely to be watching your house."

"Well we both wear the same size clothes so we could just pick up some stuff there."

"I would really like to take a look inside both of your homes to see if there is any evidence that they have been there looking for anything. So here's what we will do. After dark we will drive out to your house Molly. Ill act like I'm doing a regular check out of the house. Once I've decided that everything is ok, then Donna can go in and get what you need." The sheriff says.

"Great." I said.

"I'm sure the house is going to be locked up, so how do we get in?" The sheriff asks.

"There is a key under the flowerpot on the front porch." Molly says.

"You do understand that if the Colonel catches us, and wants to know why we are getting your clothes, I will have to tell him where you are and he will probably come get you."

"I understand." I replied.

"Can't you get a federal judge or someone to say that the colonel can't take us? I mean there has to be away to protect us without the colonel locking us up and separating us from our family." I said.

"Well to get a federal judge we would have to drive to Oklahoma City and that is a very bad place to drive to right now. Plus the Colonel is a part of a task force appointed by the president. I'm not sure a judge, even a federal one, would want to try and go up against him. You would also have to convince the judge that someone like the colonel wanting to protect you and your family is a bad thing. Like I told you last night, you staying here is just a temporary detour to give me some time to figure out what to do."

Once again we hear a car door slam and the sheriff looks out to see who it is.

"It's Murphy."

The deputy walks up to the door and the sheriff lets him in.

"Well that was interesting." Murphy says.

"What did you find out?" The sheriff asks?

"Well the writing is definitely Chinese. It's notes that one of them wrote down about the girls. About what the girls said, things that they were supposed to say and ask the girls, and different ways to try to get them to talk. It also says that they were convinced that Abby was lying and knew where the laptop was. It says in big letters, if there is nothing on the laptop then why is she trying to keep us from finding it. It also says that if they determined that the girls did know something they were to bring them with them when they came back."

"Came back where?" The sheriff asks.

"I don't know. The only place that is mentioned is Tulsa, but that is in regards to where the two Americans that they paid to act like the Steven's were going to say they were from."

"I can't believe this." I said.

"You're saying that it was actually the Chinese that were holding us out there?"

"Looks that way." The sheriff says.

"We should have enough information with this to get an arrest warrant for the Steven's and whomever else you can identify." The sheriff says.

"Take this stuff over to the courthouse and see if you can get the judge to issue an arrest warrant." The sheriff tells Murphy.

"I'll get right on it."

"In the morning I'm going to take a ride out to see the colonel. I have to tell him about this, but I know he is going to start asking questions about how I got a hold of this info, and if you two were already gone when I got there, and stuff like that. I can't lie to him so I'm not sure how I'm going to handle this."

CHAPTER SEVENTEEN

A NOTE IN THE PARK

I think this was one of the most boring days I've ever spent, but now it was dark and the sheriff is getting ready to go to Molly's house.

"You two make sure you stay away from the windows and don't answer the door if anybody knocks."

"We won't." I said.

"We should be back in about an hour y'all help yourself to whatever's in the fridge."

The sheriff and Donna leave and as soon as they are out of sight I say to Molly, "Ok how far are we from the town square?"

"About two blocks." Molly says. "It's over one street and down a block why."

"We need to go there and get back before they do." I said.

"What are you talking about?" Molly asks.

"Well Shane is probably hiding out from everyone since he was able to give the colonel the slip. So I want to go to the Hopes and Dreams Statue to see if he left a note."

"Do you really think he went to a public park and put a note there for you?"

"Yes I do. Just like we are going to the public park and see if he did. I need to find a pen and a piece of paper to write a note for him."

I look around and find a note pad and pen. I write a short note saying I'm staying at the sheriff's house.

"Let's go." I said.

"I think we should go out the back door in case someone is watching." Molly says.

They slip out the back door and make their way down through the woods until they get to the street.

"Walk normally so no one will notice us."

"There is no one around so I don't think that will be a problem." Molly says.

As we make our way to the park a car starts coming toward us.

"Oh crap, head into the park by the trees." I said.

We dart into the park and out of sight. The car pulls up and stops next to where we are. It sets there for a few minutes and then drives off.

"Wow! I thought they were going to come after us." Molly says.

"Let's go." I said.

We finally make it to the statue and I check the hiding place. There's a note. I unfold it and read it out loud.

"It says, Trust no one. I'm at the school computer lab".

"Let me see" Molly says and takes the note from me. I quickly take the note I had written and put it in the hiding place. I take the note from Molly and tare it into a thousand pieces.

"No one will be able to read that. Let's head back to the sheriffs house."

The return trip went a lot faster; as a matter of fact we ran most of the way. When we got to the street in front of the house we stopped dead in our tracks. There were two men in suits standing on the front porch waiting for someone to answer the door.

"That doesn't look good." I said.

One of the men walks off the porch and walks around to the back of the house. He returns and they both get in their car.

"Molly that's the same car we saw by the square." I said.

The car backs out of the driveway and pulls down the road and parks.

"Great! They are watching the house so how are we supposed to get back to it?" Molly asks.

"How far is the school from here?" I ask.

"About ten blocks." Molly replies.

"Let's go." I said. "Wait! Wait!"

The sheriff and Donna drive up into the front yard. They get out of the car and walk to the front door. Donna has both arms full of clothes and the sheriff has a brown bag in his arm.

The sheriff pauses as Donna goes in the door to see who is pulling up in the driveway. The car pulls in and the two men get out. They walk up to the sheriff and one of them sticks out his hand to shake the sheriff's hand. They exchange some words back and forth and then all three go into the house.

"What the heck is that all about?" I ask.

"I don't know but it looks like the sheriff was expecting them. So what do you want to do?" Molly asks.

"Let's wait until they leave and then go back over there." I said.

"I'm freezing I hope they don't take long." Molly says.

"I'll just tell the sheriff that we got out of the house when they showed up and waited outside until they left." I said.

"That won't be totally untrue."

"What about Shane?" Molly asks.

"We have to figure out a way to go over to the school and see if he's there." I said.

"Then what?"

"We need to get him and his parents and our parents back together."

"How?"

"I don't know. One thing that is really bothering me is the whole <u>trust no one</u> part of his note. You know Shane he wouldn't have said that if there wasn't a very good reason."

"Do you think he even meant the sheriff?" Molly asks.

"He said no one."

"Well we have to trust someone. We are too young to drive so we can't get anywhere without walking or someone driving us. We can't walk because we are "Americas most wanted" and everyone will see us. Perry doesn't have a bus or any form of public transportation. The one cab in town doesn't run half the time and it takes money to ride in it when it does. And oh, we don't have any money." Molly says.

"I thought we could trust the sheriff but I'm not so sure now. I mean he obviously knew these guys were coming over and he never mentioned it or warned us about it. Plus I think he is going to try to get us to go see the colonel in the morning."

The front door to the sheriff's house opens up and the sheriff and the two men walk out.

"I wish we could hear what they were saying. Let's try to get closer." I said.

The two men look very serious and don't appear to be buying whatever the sheriff is saying but they extend their hand to shake and then walk to the car.

"As soon as they get out of sight we go back in the house." I said.

"Let's go around to the back door."

As they walk up on the back porch the back door opens and there stands the sheriff.

"You girl's come back in you must be freezing out there."

"Yea it's really cold out here." Molly says.

"So who were those guys?" I ask.

"They were from Homeland Security the sheriff says."

"Really." I said.

"I think they are pretty convinced that you two are staying here, but seemed to be a lot more interested in where Shane might be."

"Why?" I ask.

Donna walks into the living room caring a platter with four cups of hot chocolate on it.

"Here you guy's drink this so you can warm up," she says.

"Why do they want Shane?" I ask again.

"They think he is in great danger. They said if one of these groups get him they will smuggle him out of here and do whatever it takes to get him to tell them how the virus works. Once they get the information he will be of no use to them anymore and they will dispose of him to keep anybody else from getting to him."

"I'm sure our government feels the same way right?" I ask.

"What do you mean?" The sheriff asks.

"I think it's pretty obvious. Shane has the knowledge to write a virus that no one else has been able to. This virus, if used as a weapon, could plunge whole countries into chaos and disrupt their military, their government, and their people's ability to survive. Then the government wielding the virus would have the ability to come in and take over or at least inflict some serious damage to that country. Correct?"

"I guess so." The sheriff says.

"So you have to think that our own government would love to have that knowledge and would not want to share it with anybody. Right? Now we have a twelve-year-old boy who not only has that knowledge but also accidentally proved that it would work. So our government grabs that boy and that boy tells them his secret, and now our government has that power. This is great because for the most part our government does what's right and they are not really looking to conquer some other country. However they do have a serious problem. What do they do with the kid? They can't let him go home. One of the other countries might grab him while he's out feeding his horse and take him away and learn the secret. I don't think they

126

would <u>dispose</u> of him but they might lock him away in some base somewhere until time marches on and his earth shaking technology becomes old and useless just like the CD player. So I think I just figured out why Shane split from the ranch and why he said trust no one. He doesn't want to live the next ten years locked away like some lab rat."

"Wow. You sure your only twelve?" The sheriff says. "You must have given this a lot of thought?"

"Actually I just thought of it while I was standing outside waiting on those men to leave." I said.

"Well, I have to say you make perfect sense."

"It really is starting to make sense. The colonel wants the secret. The terrorist and bad foreign countries want the secret. Shane has the secret. Molly and I are Shane's close friends and they all think that we have Shane's laptop or maybe even Shane has told us the secret. The colonel really wants to protect our families and us but he also knows that keeping our parents locked away is kind of like bait to draw us out. He doesn't want anything to happen to the secret."

"Abby, I have to agree with you, but there is another side to the coin. I mean, I know where you are going with this. You're going to say that the only way we can save Shane and even yourselves is to give the <u>secret</u> to everybody so no one would be able to benefit from it right." The sheriff says.

"Exactly." I said.

"But think about this, the other side of the coin. Let's say that our government gets the secret and keeps it from being used against us or anybody else. Your right, Shane disappears for a long time. Maybe even the two of you, depending on what you know, but the U.S. has the <u>secret</u> the <u>virus</u> and maybe even the antivirus that will stop it. Now we know that North Korea for instance is trying to build nuclear weapons. We also know that they will use those weapons against the United States and its allies. What if they start to do just that? What if they start to launch those weapons against us? This virus could shut them down completely. Give the U.S. and our allies the chance to go in and destroy all their facilities thereby saving hundreds of thousands of American lives and since we don't have to bomb them probably a lot of North Korean lives also. Wouldn't that be worth it? Shane is not going to be tortured. He would probably be put somewhere where him and his family would be taken care of. He would probably end up having access to computers and equipment that he would never have access to in the normal world."

"I can see what you are saying." I said. "But he wouldn't be free and he should be the one that makes that decision. He should decide if he wants to give up his freedom. Not me, you, or the colonel. And you know as well as I do. If the colonel, or homeland security, get him, he will never be given that opportunity. It's too important to the government. They will do whatever is necessary to get what they want. Besides, he's just a twelve-year-old boy; they know what's best for him. Right?"

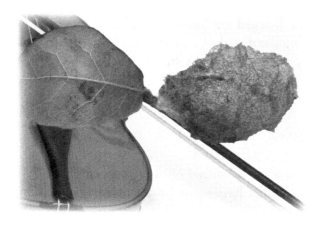

CHAPTER EIGHTEEN

NO HIP HOP COCOON

After being up half the night debating with the sheriff we finally got to go to bed.

"Before you go to sleep will you tell me if you have a plan?" Molly asks.

"I still don't have one. I just know we have to find Shane and see what he wants to do. How are we going to do that without telling someone? I don't know. Right now I just want to sleep so I'm going to let Lindsey put me in a deep tranquil state and then I'm going to sleep like a baby. But first I need to delete this bad track so that I don't die in my sleep when it comes on. Track four "Cocoon" gone. It's still there. One more time track 4 "cocoon" gone. Nope."

"That means you're going to have to reformat the thing to get rid of it." Molly says.

"Nice."

"Why don't you just un-check it in your play list?" Molly asks.

"Duh. That's why I have you. To handle the hard stuff."

"I just listened to hours of debate come from you that would have dazzled them on the floor of the Senate and you can't even work an iPod." Molly says.

"Good night Miss Tanton."

"Goodnight Miss Tate."

Later.

"Molly you still awake?" I ask.

"Sort of." Molly replies.

"You have all of Lindsey Stirling's music right?"

"You couldn't have waited until morning to ask me that?" Molly replies.

"Do you remember any of her songs being named cocoon?"

"No, but it sounds like something she would name a song."

"Do you have a song by her named cocoon or have you ever heard of a song by her or anybody else named cocoon?"

"No I haven't."

"Molly what is a cocoon?"

"It's a thing that protects a caterpillar while it . . . turns . . . . into . . . . A . . . . butterfly!" Molly quietly yells.

Both of them jump up out of bed.

"It's not a song it's a program that's why it won't play on the iPod. It's some kind of software program." I said.

There jubilation is disturbed by an escalating argument coming from another part of the house. The sheriff and Donna seem to be having a small disagreement.

"You don't have to do that!" Donna yells.

We move closer to the door as to hear better what is being said.

"Do you really grasp what's going on here?" The sheriff in and increasingly louder voice asks. "These aren't two runaway kids we have here. These girls are in serious danger and that puts you, me, and anyone else that gets in the way in danger."

"Brett, you know if you turn them over to the colonel no one will ever see them again." Donna says. "And why are you so sure they know where Shane is?"

"I don't, but Abby seems to be hiding something. She said something a little out of place earlier that makes me think she has been in communication with him. Besides those two guys from Homeland Security swear they saw them at the park."

"What'd she say?" Donna asks.

"It wasn't so much what she said but how she said it and it was when she said Shane split from the ranch and he said trust no one. It was in the context of <u>he split</u> and <u>then</u> said, <u>don't trust anyone</u>. No one supposedly knows where he is and no one has seen him since he <u>split</u> yesterday. We aren't even supposed to know that he split, yet Abby claims he said don't trust anyone." The sheriff says.

"Oh my God you over think everything." Donna says.

"That's my job." The sheriff says.

"They are just kids for God's sake. They grew up right here in town. They grew up trusting you as the sheriff to protect them. That's your job also."

I walk into the room where the sheriff and Donna are standing.

"I'm sorry Abby. We didn't mean for you" . . .

I cut Donna off.

"I do know where he is." I said.

"What?" The sheriff says.

"I do know where Shane is. I know where the laptop is. Yes I have had word from him sense he split." I said.

"Abby, don't say another word." Donna says.

"It's ok." I said.

"No, she's right, don't say another word. We don't need that information and if you tell us anymore there is no way I could just set on the information." The sheriff says.

"Why did you just tell us that?" Donna asks.

"I was listening to what you said and your right. I grew up trusting that the sheriff, a good friend of my fathers since they were in grade school, was protecting me and my family. I still believe that. So sheriff, what are you going to do?" I said.

"The first thing we have to do is retrieve the laptop and anything else that might be of interest to them. Then we have to get the three of you as far away from here as we can." The sheriff says.

"The <u>three</u> of us? I ask.

"Yea. You, Molly and Shane."

"I don't know that Shane will go for that. I will have to ask him if he is ok with it before I let you know where he's at."

"How do you do that?" Molly asks.

"I will go see him."

"How? If you try to walk there someone will surely see you." The sheriff says.

"Donna can drive us. That way you won't know where we went and if Shane doesn't go along with it he will have time to move before you sweet talk it out of her."

"I told you I don't want to know where he's at." The sheriff says.

"Well when do we go?" Donna asks.

"First thing in the morning." The sheriff says.

"I'll pull your car in the garage so the girls can get in it without anyone seeing them. I'll leave at the same time you do and maybe they will follow me because they think I'm the one that knows where you are. Then you can drive wherever you need to. I hope this doesn't blow up in our face because I'm sure they will charge Donna and me with some sort of treason."

Once again we try to go to sleep.

"Abby?" Molly asks.

"Yes." I reply.

"Why did you decide to trust them?"

"Well I figure worse case they give us up to the colonel and we end up hid out somewhere until this all goes away. I figure that's better than Shane trying to survive out there and one of the bad guys finally finding him and taking him away. I mean he can't survive out there forever. This way we at least tried to help him. And I believe the sheriff is sincere. I think he is trying to do the right thing. The problem is that this is one of those times when the right thing is not right for everybody."

"Do you think Shane will go along with us on this?" Molly asks.

"No. I don't think he will. I think he will be very angry with us. But what are you going do?" I said. "Don't let me forget to gather up some food to take him in the morning. He probably hasn't eaten anything in a while."

Molly gets up and walks over to Abby's bed.

"Scoot over." Molly says.

I slide over in the bed and Molly sits down on the side of the bed.

"I know your laying here trying to figure out the next move so let me help. Let's talk this through." Molly says. "Do you think the program we discovered on your iPod is something he was working on to fix stuff or is it actually the Monarch program?"

"I don't know. I think if it was the Monarch program he would have called it that. I don't think he was thinking that anybody was going to be grabbing his stuff so he wasn't trying to hide anything at that point. It has to be a fix. But did he finish it and can it be used from an iPod or do we need the original?" I said.

"We need to go to your house and get the CD." Molly says.

"And the laptop." I said.

"The laptop is at your house?" Molly says.

"Yep."

"You knew where the laptop was all this time?"

"Yep."

"Those Chinese people could have killed us to get it and you actually knew where it was. Un freaking believable."

"What?" I said.

"There isn't anything on it. We could have died over a laptop that has nothing on it."

"Can we change the subject?" I ask. "Did you hear that?"

"What?" Molly says.

"Listen. There it is again. Someone is tapping on the window."

"Oh crap." Molly says.

"I'll wake up the sheriff."

"No wait." I said.

"Wait, are you nuts?" Molly says.

"Terrorists don't knock. Or tap on windows." I said.

"Sure they don't, unless they are trying to trick someone into opening the window." Molly says.

"I'll go to the window and see who it is. If someone grabs me you start screaming and wake up Donna and the sheriff."

I start slowly walking toward the window. The tapping gets louder. I pull the curtain open a little bit and then I open it all the way.

"Oh My God it's Shane. Help me open the window."

Shane crawls in through the window.

"Be quiet they will hear you." Molly says.

Shane finally gets in and I hug him like he's never been hugged before.

"Are you ok?" I ask him.

"I'm ok I guess." Shane says.

"Are y'all ok?"

"We are now." I said.

"Why are you here at the sheriff's house?" Shane asks.

"Well it's a long story and we will fill you in later. I know you said not to trust anyone but you can trust the sheriff and his wife." I said.

"No you can't." Shane says.

"Well we really don't have any choice at this point."

"Yes we do." Shane says.

"No we don't; listen to me.

"So what is going on right now? Why are you here, where are your parents, do you have anything to eat?" Shane says.

Molly, go to the kitchen and get something for him to eat and some tea or milk or something."

"Ok." Molly says and leaves.

"Set down on the bed. Wow. I can't believe your here." I said.

"I can't believe I'm alive." Shane says.

"How did you two get caught up in this Shane asks? You guys had nothing to do with it."

"We went out to your house looking for you and I found your laptop. Then two people showed up pretending to be your grandparents, and then the Chinese kidnapped us."

"What? Can you slow down a little?"

Molly comes back in with a sandwich and a glass of milk. Shane starts devouring it.

"How long has it been since you had anything to eat?" Molly asks.

"Two and a half days."

"You said you got my laptop." Shane says.

"Yes I have it hidden in the barn at my house." I said.

"That's great because it has everything on it. The virus, the antivirus that I was working on when they grabbed me, everything." Shane says.

"Wow, I'm glad we didn't turn it over to them aren't you Molly"

"Yes I'm very glad Abby." Molly says.

"So you were working on an antivirus?" I said.

"Yes."

"The cocoon?"

"Yes. You got the disk to?"

"Yep."

"That's great. When the feds brought in my computer from the house I just knew they were going to get everything they were looking for when they found the disk. I saved nothing to the hard drive on it but put it on the CD."

"So you haven't given the colonel or anybody the software or code or whatever?"

"No. I was going to but then I figured out that they would have to make me disappear so I wouldn't give it to them. I can't really blame them they wouldn't really have a choice. I feel like a traitor." Shane says.

"You're not a traitor." I said.

"Ok it's 2:00 am. Let's try and get some sleep."

"Ok I'll get out of here." Shane says.

"No you want." I said.

"You can sleep on this bed and Molly and I will sleep on that one. In the morning we will figure out what to do. We will stay in here until the sheriff leaves and then Donna can fix us a nice breakfast."

"I hope you're right about these people because if you're not were history."

"Just trust me." I said.

CHAPTER NINETEEN

LET'S USE THE MARS ROVER

Once again my deep sleep is disturbed by a god awful sounding alarm clock. Once I'm awake I immediately think of Shane and the fact that they hadn't warned him about the alarm clock. As softly as possible, while half asleep, I call Shane. They hear a very weak "what the heck was that" from Shane and Molly jumps out of bed to guard the door.

"That's their ideal of an alarm clock." Molly says.

"Just lay there and be quiet until the sheriff is gone." I said.

In about fifteen minutes we hear them stirring around and start to smell coffee.

"It want be long now." I said.

"I hope he doesn't need to talk to us before he leaves." I said.

"I just hope he leaves instead of waiting for us to leave." Molly says.

"I just hope I can take a bath." Shane says.

"Me too. I mean, I hope you can to. You're starting to get pretty ripe there." Molly says.

"How rude, but true." I said.

After about another fifteen minutes they hear the sheriff leave.

"Well this is it. Shane you stay in here until we tell her what's going on." I said.

They walk into the kitchen and Donna is getting breakfast ready.

"Good morning ladies and I'm sorry about that alarm clock again." Donna says.

"That's fine." I said.

"I figure we will have some breakfast and then we can leave. Have you decided how we are going to do this yet?" Donna asks.

"Well we have had a change of plan. We don't need to go find Shane." I said.

"What do you mean?" Donna asks.

"Well, he's here."

"He's here?" Donna asks. "At the house?"

"Yep." I reply.

"Where is he?"

"He's in the bedroom."

"I'm going to skip the whole how did he get in and when did he get here and just go straight to the wow I don't believe this."

"Yep he's here." I said.

"Well, are you going to leave him in the bedroom or are you going to bring him in here so he can eat and we can decide the next move?"

"Shane, come on in here!" I yell.

Shane walks into the kitchen looking very much like a terrified twelve-year-old boy.

"Good morning Mrs. Hardery." Shane says.

"Come on in and sit down. You can call me Donna. The sheriff's mother is Mrs. Hardery." Donna chuckles.

"Are you hungry?"

"Very." Shane says.

"How about some pancakes and bacon?"

"Sounds great." Shane replies as his eyes light up.

"Would it be possible for me to clean up a little first? I haven't had a bath in two weeks." Shane says.

"Sure you can. Molly, show him where the restroom is. I will throw your clothes in the washer while you're taking a bath."

"Thanks." Shane says.

Shane gets up and goes to take a bath.

"He looks very scared and almost ready to give up." Donna says.

"I think he is just so afraid of what's going to happen to him. He just can't trust anybody." I said.

"Well he seems to have trusted you. Instead of hiding somewhere he's here and he wouldn't be if he didn't trust you."

"Well I hope I don't let him down."

"I think you are doing the right thing. Now we just have to figure out how to pull it off. I'm going to be honest with you, I kind of think we need to figure out a way to push this secret y'all keep talking about out to everyone on the planet." Donna says.

"Really. You really believe that?" I ask.

"Yes I do. And Abby, so does the sheriff."

"Really?"

"Yep. He told me that last night."

"Wow. That's great."

"He also told me that when I found out that Shane was ok I'm supposed to call him on the radio and ask him what time he will be home. That's a signal. Once he hears that signal he is going to go by and tell his niece to tell Shane's parents that he's ok."

"Wow that's great." I said.

Molly joins in on a high five with me.

"The sheriff said he was going to stay out in town until I called him and told him dinner was ready. That way no one would be coming by here to talk to him and you would feel a little safer. Of course he didn't know we had the extra company."

"Now do you think your genius friend in there can figure out a way to send this out to the world?" Donna asks.

"I hope he can, but even if he has an antidote there still is the problem of determining what, if anything, Internet wise, is still alive."

"I'm sure the military has recovered enough so they can operate. What about the thing up there in space the uh Space Station?" Donna says.

"The International Space Station?" Molly asks.

"You know they have to be able to communicate to it and I'm sure they have computers that are working." Donna adds.

"There is also Curiosity, the new rover that's on Mars. It surely has working computers." I said.

Shane walks out of the restroom while drying his hair with a towel.

"We have to use them both." Shane says.

"What?" I said.

"We have to use them both. The International Space Station and Curiosity. One to broadcast to the world that the fix is available and one to transmit the antivirus."

"Explain." I said.

"Can I get some of that bacon and those pancakes first?"

"Coming right up." Donna says.

"Thanks for washing my clothes Mrs. Hardery."

"You're welcome." Donna replies.

"Would you like milk or coffee?" She asks.

"Can I have both?"

"Sure, do you like your milk with Nestles Quick or straight up?" Donna asks.

"Straight up please."

"Before you get started explaining stuff I need to tell you guys something. Brett wanted to make sure you were aware of this in case something happened.

We, like a lot of people here in tornado alley, have a storm cellar. We use it for food storage mostly but we have on occasion used it when tornados have touched down in the area. Ours is a little different than most peoples because your sheriff can be a little weird. He is one of those people that think that one day we will have to defend our food and lives from our neighbors, during the end times if you will. Or, maybe something like what is going on right now. So the entrance to our cellar is totally hidden. If you go into the laundry room you will notice that the clothes hamper is setting on a rug. If you slide the hamper and the rug to the right you will find a door in the floor. Pull it up and you can go down steps into the cellar. Once you are down there you push the steps back up and that slides the rug and hamper back in place. Pretty cool until you need a jar of pickles then it's a pain in the butt. It is also wired for sound. On the back wall, setting on the table is a speaker. If you turn it on you can hear what's going on in the house."

"That's so cool." Molly says.

"That's really weird." I said.

"Why are you telling us this?" Shane asks.

"The sheriff feels that it's just a matter of time until the colonel or someone worse decides to check this place out to see if you're here. If that time comes and you want to hide then that should be a pretty good place. He decided to tell ya'll about it after you had to stand outside in the cold when the Homeland Security guys were here."

Donna takes everyone's order as to the number of pancakes and starts flipping them on the grill. As she starts dishing them out she says, "Ok Shane how do we do this?"

"Well I don't have it all figured out, but I think I have figured out a way. The Mars rover right now is setting on Mars with nothing to do. NASA and JPL have bigger fish to fry right now with the crisis that's going on. The rover has a magnificent data and communications system that receives and transmits data very reliably and very quickly. The data is in TCPIP format."

"It's in what?" I said.

"TCP\IP is an anagram for Transmission Control Protocol slash Internet Protocol."

"Is that a good thing?" I ask.

"It's a very good thing. It is the common set of rules and regulations that everyone uses to transmit stuff over the network. So if I can figure out a way to uplink my antivirus, the cocoon, to the rover I can then command it to start retransmitting it every thirty seconds or so. I'm sure that JPL probably pushes that information through satellites in orbit all around the earth so that they can maintain communications at all times. So we can pass the antivirus to each of these satellites as it relays through them. Now, based on the distance from earth to mars right now, it takes about fourteen minutes for a command to reach the rover from earth, so by the time they figure out what we did it will take at least fourteen minutes before they can shut it down. If I'm lucky and I figure out how they are doing things I can tell it to ignore any shut down command for the next x number of hours. I don't want to keep it tied up to long just in case it is supposed to do something else and it ignores their command and ends up driving off a cliff or something. I have enough stuff on my resume now, with shutting down the Internet, I don't need to add destroying a two and a half billion dollar mars rover.

The second problem is how we let the world know that the Curiosity Rover is transmitting the fix. The International Space Station has a ham radio system on board that the astronauts use to talk to school children, amateur astronomers, and really anyone that can get through. It also receives APRS formatted packets and can retransmit them. There are thousands of ham radio operators that monitor it constantly. Or least they did until they lost power. Luckily a lot of those guys are geeks and have solar powered radios or generators to run them on just in case. But you can bet that every government in the world has someone somewhere that is listening to it. If we can broadcast a message to it, it will be received and re-transmitted before they can figure out what we did. If enough people here it they can spread it around all over the world. All we really need is for one major country to get it, or hopefully our government gets it, and then they will be under pressure to use it. When people start finding out that there is a fix and it is freely available the pressure on the government from the people will be enormous. It will still take a long time to fix everything but at least it will be a start."

"So how do we send this up to the Space Station?" Donna asks.

"That's the part I haven't completely worked out yet. We need a transmitter and a good yagi antenna. The transmitter has to be able to transmit data packets. Most ham radios operators today run what I think is called the AMPRNet or use a terminal node controller that will allow you to hook a terminal or even a computer into them and use them sort of like a teletype to send text back and forth between stations."

"So where can we find this set up?" Donna asks.

"Will Pastor Gleason's ham radio do it?" I ask.

"No, he has an older station. It would work for the space station broadcast."

"What's that guy's name that lives out by where the Old Rose Hill School used to be, you know the one that has all those antennas on his pickup and that big dish behind his house?" I ask.

"Andy something." Donna says.

"Andy Records." Shane says.

"Yea that's him. Surely he has the right stuff. He repairs all the radios for the county and the hospital." Donna says.

"He definitely has the right equipment but he would never do it. He is an ex-Navy guy and very pro-military. He would want our military to control the virus and the antivirus and never let us send it out to everyone." Shane says.

"Well maybe the sheriff could convince him." Donna says.

"Maybe, but I have a friend that lives on a farm near Oklahoma City, he has the equipment and would gladly let us use it." Shane says.

"You're talking about Eric Hill right?" I said.

"That's him. I'm sure he would help, and my dad gave him a bunch of solar energy equipment to run his stuff off of about a year ago."

"So we have two possibilities. I think we should let the sheriff in on this and see what he thinks." Donna says.

"Isn't it a little early to call him and tell him that dinner is ready? I mean it's only eight in the morning." I said.

"Yea we really didn't figure out a code for come home right now." Donna says.

"I'll call him and tell him to come home early for dinner because we have things to do this evening." Donna says.

"He will get the come home early for dinner part. If not I'll go find him and bring him home."

CHAPTER TWENTY

You're Welcome Anytime

It only took about fifteen minutes and the sheriff pulled into the driveway. When he walked in and saw Shane setting there he took off his cowboy hat and threw it on the couch.

"Wow. I really didn't expect to see you here Shane."

"Well it was all kind of sudden." Shane says.

"Kind of sudden. You spent the night here." Donna says while chuckling.

"You really need to install a security system sheriff." I said.

"I guess I do." The sheriff says.

"So what is the latest?" The sheriff asks.

"Well, Shane has a way to fix the Monarch Virus and get himself, Abby, and Molly off the three most wanted list." Donna says.

"Ok, what's the plan?" The sheriff asks.

"Well, without going through the details as to how this is going to fix things, Shane can you skip to the part that involves us, the sheriff and I." Donna says.

"Sure. First we need you to take us to Abby's house to retrieve my laptop."

"I doubt seriously if it is still there." The sheriff says.

"Why's that?" I ask.

"They have gone through every inch of your house looking for it; if it was there I'm sure they found it."

"Well it's not actually in the house, it's in the barn." I said.

"I'm sure they probably looked there also." The sheriff says.

"Well, if the laptop isn't there then we need to get the CD that has the antivirus on it and that's in my room."

"If it wasn't a factory CD of some kind they probably took it. Anything that had been burned by you would be suspect and they would take it and see what was on it." The sheriff says.

"Wonderful, it just gets better and better." Molly says.

"Let's hope they just saw the Lindsey Stirling tracks on the CD and thought it was a mix and ignored the track that had the cocoon on it." I said.

"So if they are both gone are we out of luck?" Donna asks.

"Well, the only other chance we have is trying to pull it off Abby's iPod." Shane says. "I'm not sure how the iPod stored it. It could be usable with a little work, or a bunch of unusable gibberish and a total loss. If it's lost the only thing I could do is re-write it and to do that I will need a computer and some special software. Even if we have to try and take it off Abby's iPod I will still need a computer."

"We need to go over there and see if anything is left?" I said.

"Well that is going to take some planning itself. The colonel has a couple of his men taking care of the livestock at both your places and we will have to go to Abby's place while they are at Shane's place." The sheriff says.

"Since there is one of your radios in my car, you could set at the end of the road and watch for them and alert us if they start heading our way." Donna says.

"I'll go out ahead of you and see where they are and give you a heads up when they leave Abby's and head for Shane's.

I'm assuming they do Shane's place after they do Abby's but I'm not sure." The sheriff says.

"We are going to have to come up with a code to use on the radio because they will be listening." Donna says.

"Ok let's assume we get your laptop or the CD then what" The sheriff asks.

"If we get the stuff, then we need to see if Andy Records will let us use his Ham Radio system to upload it to the mars rover." Shane says.

"The MARS ROVER. You're kidding right! Please tell me you're kidding?" The sheriff says.

"And the International Space Station." I said.

"Right. Sure. The rover and the space station. You're tired of destroying things here on earth so you're branching out to outer space." The sheriff says.

"That's mean." I said.

"How rude Brett!" Donna says.

"It's okay. I might as well get used to it. When the word gets out it was me people are going to be a lot meaner to me." Shane says.

"I'm sorry the sheriff says but you can't just expect me to jump right in and go along with you when you're planning on committing a few federal offenses that I'm pretty sure are felonies."

"Just settle down Brett, he's not going to break anything, he is just going to use them to retransmit the data to the world." Donna says.

"Oh good, we are probably only looking at ten years instead of twenty." The sheriff says.

"I'm onboard with this, so you can either get onboard, or leave and go write some parking tickets because we are going to do it." Donna says. "If I remember right you were all for them sending the fix to everyone in the world last night?"

"I'm all for it, but are you sure this is the only way, I mean there has to be another way."

"There may be, but we don't know what it is and we don't have time to sit around and come up with another one." Donna says.

"Ok. The first problem you have with your plan, if I heard you correctly, you are planning on using Andy Records equipment." The sheriff says. "You might as well try seeing if the colonel will let you use his equipment."

"I suggested him because I know he has the proper equipment and he is close. I would actually prefer to see if Eric Hill would help us out, but he lives just outside of Oklahoma City and it would be extremely difficult to get there." Shane says.

"Ok let's assume we get the stuff from Abby's house, and we get Andy to go along with us, then what? Please don't tell me we have to kidnap the President or something like that." The sheriff says.

"No, we transmit the signal to the rover while we simultaneously talk to the Space Station and transmit some packets to it. Then we wait to see if anyone was able to receive the retransmitted signals, and if they did, then we succeeded. We set back and wait for our government as well as the other governments to call off the dogs so to speak." Shane says.

"All right, I guess I'm onboard. I am going to call one of my deputies and have him come over here. You three will have to go down into the cellar. When he gets here I'm going to tell him to check out your houses and see if anyone is there and then have him set up the road and watch for anyone coming that way. I can't tell him this over the radio so he will have to come here." The sheriff says.

"I guess we need to clean up these dishes and cups so he doesn't see them and get suspicious." Donna says.

"He may be in the neighborhood, so you three go ahead and head for the cellar." The sheriff walks over and picks up the radio mic and calls deputy Murphy.

"Base calling Murphy you copy?" The sheriff says.

"This is Murphy go ahead."

"I need you to swing by the house as soon as you can."

"Roger that I'm about ten minutes away."

"Ok he is on his way. Let's make sure there is nothing lying around that would indicate we have company."

"He knows were here. Remember he was there when you picked us up." I said.

"True but he doesn't know that Shane's here and the less he knows the better."

Molly, Shane, and I head back down into the cellar. A few minutes later they hear the deputy come in.

"What's up boss?" Deputy Murphy asks.

"I need you to do a little recon work for me first thing in the morning." The sheriff says.

"Ok what you got?"

"That Colonel Krom has a couple of his men taking care of the Tate's place and the Bevil's place. I think they are just taking care of the animals, but I need to know when they are there and when they leave. I also need you to watch and see if anyone else is visiting either place. Just check around and see what's happening. Give me a call on the radio when they are gone and just say the road is now clear. Then I need you to block it off at the beginning of the road and let me know when someone starts down it."

"Ok no problem. That's the Shadow Lane end right?" The deputy asks.

"Yea, I am going to park down on the other end by the Bevil's place."

"So what's up?" The deputy asks.

"The less you know the better off you will be, but I need Donna to check out something at the Tate place and I don't want anyone dropping in on her while she's there." The sheriff says.

"No problem, so if someone starts down the road while she's there, you want me to stop them?"

"Yep, stop them and give me a call on the radio saying something like <u>sheriff I have whoever stopped tell me when it's clear</u> then hold them until she has time to get out of there."

"What if they ask what is going on, what do I tell them?" The deputy asks.

"Just tell them something is blocking the road and they have to wait until it's clear. That will be the truth because we will be blocking the road." The sheriff says.

"No problem, what time do you want me to do this?"

"Let's start at seven in the morning."

As they are talking they hear car doors slamming in the front yard. The sheriff walks to the front door and looks out side.

"Great, that's all I need. Deputy you get out of here right now. I'll call you first thing in the morning."

"Shouldn't I stay here and see what they want?" The deputy asks.

"Go! Right now!" The sheriff says.

The deputy walks out the front door as the colonel walks up to the front door and asks to come in. The deputy turns and walks back in. Five of Krom's men start looking around the outside of the house.

"Colonel Krom. What brings you by?" The sheriff asks.

"I think you know why I'm here." The colonel says.

"No, actually I don't, but you're welcome to come in."

"So where have you stashed my three detainees?"

"Detainees, I'm not sure I follow." The sheriff says.

"Don't play games with me sheriff or I'll have your badge before you can say treason." The colonel says.

Two of the men come in from the outside and tell the colonel that everything is clear outside and the colonel tells them to check the inside of the house.

"Whoa wait a minute. I haven't seen any kind of search warrant or anything and you can't just walk in here and search my home." The sheriff says.

"Yea I can sheriff; I can do anything I desire."

"I don't think so."

"Don't push me sheriff." The colonel says.

The deputy steps between the sheriff and the colonel.

"I believe the sheriff is right colonel. This is still a free country, so to speak, and you need a warrant to search this property." The deputy says.

"Ok, just everyone stand down and let's not get into some kind of pushing contest." The sheriff says.

"Deputy you just go ahead and leave. I would be happy to escort these men around the house so they can look and verify that whatever it is they are looking for isn't here. I have nothing to hide so if you allow me to escort them you can look, if not, then we are going to have a real problem and you may have the authority to search this place without a warrant but one of us will be assessing that from a hospital room."

The colonel tells his men to stand down.

"I will play along sheriff, as a matter of fact; you can escort me while I have a look around." The colonel says.

"You two men return to your vehicle." The colonel says.

"Right this way colonel." The sheriff says.

They walk into the utility room and out into the garage.

"Does this look ok to you colonel?"

"Fine." The colonel says."

They then walk back into the house and check out the bathroom and the bedrooms.

"This look ok?" The sheriff asks.

"Fine." The colonel replies."

The sheriff opens the closets and Donna pulls back the drapes.

"Fine. Once again, I know you have them hid somewhere, and you are really making this bad on yourself sheriff." The colonel says.

"I assume you are talking about Shane Bevil and the two girls am I right?" The sheriff asks.

"You know who I'm talking about." The colonel says.

"Here's the deal sheriff, you think that you're protecting three young twelve year old kids from the evil government, but that's not the case and you're in way over your head. This young boy has information that is of vital importance to this government and we want it, we are not out to hurt anyone, just get some information. I also need the two girls because they can identify the six Chinese people we have in custody as the ones that were holding them captive out at the old airport." The colonel says.

"So that's what was going on out there. We heard a radio call and went out there and had a look around." The sheriff says.

"So you are saying that the Chinese were holding those two girls hostage out there? Wow that's crazy." The deputy says.

"You being the sheriff it would seem you would want these people prosecuted for what they did to two of your fellow citizens here in Perry." The colonel says.

"Sure I would and I'm sure they will get what's coming to them." The sheriff says.

"Well, you tell those two kids that I need them to identify these people pretty quick if they have the time to drop by the ranch." The colonel says.

Then he turns around and walks out.

"Will do." The sheriff says.

He opens the door for the colonel.

CHAPTER TWENTY-ONE

YOU CAN'T ARREST
THE SHERIFF

The colonel walks out to his car but stops to talk to two of his men. The two soldiers walk back up to the front door and walk right into the house.

"Sheriff Hardery I'm going to have to ask you to turn around and face the wall." The soldier says.

"What?" The sheriff says.

"Sir I'm placing you under arrest for the deliberate interference in a federal investigation mandated by the President of the United States."

Donna rushes over and grabs the sheriff.

"Have you people lost your mind?" Donna yells?

"Ma'am I'm going to have to ask you to step back or I'm going to arrest you also."

"Let it go honey." The sheriff says.

"I'll be fine and you have things you need to get done and you can't do that if you are locked up with me."

Donna backs up and the sheriff turns to face the wall. One of the soldier's places handcuffs on him. The other soldier grabs his arm and walks him out to their Humvee. They put the sheriff into the Humvee and drive off.

"I do not believe this." Donna says.

She turns to the utility room and tells us it's clear to come on out. We come up out of the cellar and I'm very distraught.

"I'm so sorry Donna; this has got completely out of hand." I said.

"It'll be ok." Donna says.

"We need to turn ourselves in." Shane says.

"I agree." I said.

Molly sits down on the couch and starts crying. Donna sets down by her.

"It's cool Molly. We will be ok I promise."

"Let's just walk over to the park and stand there until they pick us up." Shane says.

"Until who picks us up? The Chinese, North Koreans." I ask.

"Did you guys not hear what the sheriff said?" Donna asks.

"He said we had something we need to get done. He was talking about your plan; so don't start giving up on me now." Donna says.

"I'll call Murphy in the morning and tell him we are still a go."

Even though the windows were blacked out the sheriff was very aware that they were taking him to the ranch. *Well maybe I can bring their parents up to date on what's happening the sheriff thinks to himself. They are probably planning on just that. That's why I'm being taken out there. They want me to start talking to the Bevil's and Tate's so they can listen in and learn where they are. How stupid do they think I am the sheriff thinks?*

The Humvee pulls into the Ranch and pulls up close to the doors of one of the temporary buildings. The two soldiers get out and one opens the door.

"Please step out sir."

Once again one of the soldiers grabs his arm and they walk straight into the entrance and take an immediate left. They start down a hallway toward what the sheriff assumed would be his new home. At least for now anyway. Out of the corner of his eye he sees Erica coming out of what appears to be a restroom. The sudden expression on her face was one of <u>they arrested the sheriff</u> and <u>oh no if the sheriff has been arrested where is Abby?</u>

She starts to yell out at the sheriff but stops and heads to the room where her mother and dad are. The sheriff is placed in a room and the two soldiers abruptly turn and leave without a word. The sheriff hears the door lock as they close it behind him.

"Dad!" Erica yells as she runs into their room.

"They just brought the sheriff in."

"What?" Dad asks.

"They put him in the last room on the right, I think." Erica says.

"Why would they arrest the sheriff?" Mom asks.

"Wow, I don't know." Dad says.

"He probably wouldn't tell them where Abby is." Harlan says.

"You know son, you could be right. We know he had them at least for a while so maybe he still does and won't give them up." Dad says.

"I don't think you should be thinking out loud Jerry, you know they have this place bugged." Mom says.

"That's true. I think I'll walk down and use the restroom." Dad says.

As he walks out he runs into Henry Bevil.

"Hey have you heard anything new?" Henry asks.

"They just brought the sheriff in." Dad says.

"Really, what did they do with him?" Henry asks.

"I think he's in the last room on the right," dad says as he nods toward the end of the hall.

They both walk down to the room and dad lightly taps on the door. After a few seconds they here a "who is it" come from inside the room.

"It's Henry and Jerry. Is that you sheriff?"

"Yea it's me." The sheriff replies.

"Don't say anything right now, we will talk later." Dad says.

They turn and walk away.

"So what do you think they brought him in for?" Henry asks.

"I think it is a set up to try and learn where the kids are but I'm not really sure." Dad says.

"So how are we going to talk to him without them hearing us?" Henry asks.

"I'm not sure but we will figure something out." Dad says.

"I have some other disturbing news." Henry says.

"That soldier that's kin to the sheriff."

"Debra Penson?" Dad replies.

"Yea. She told me that they brought in six other people and put them in the other building. She recognized two of them as being my Mother in law and father in law."

"What? Dad says.

"It couldn't be them; there is no way they could have got here from Tulsa."

"It has to be the two people that came to our house and said they were Joslyn's parents." Dad says.

As they are talking the colonel appears in the hall and walks down to them.

"I need both of you to do something for me. I'm going to bring two people down here and I want you to take a look at them and see if you recognize them." The colonel says.

"Sure." They both say.

"Don't say anything until I have taken them away." The colonel says.

He then walks off.

"I have a feeling we are going to get to see the people you were talking about right now." Dad says.

About five minutes later the colonel walks down the hall with a man and woman escorted by two soldiers. Dad immediately recognizes them as Joslyn's parents. They bring the two up in front of them and have them turn completely around. The two recognize dad and start to say something and the colonel tells them there is no talking. The colonel then tells the two soldiers to take them back to their holding cells. As they walk off the colonel says "Well do either of you recognize them?"

Henry speaks first and says he has never seen them before in his life.

"Really? You have never seen you father and mother in law before." Dad says with amazement.

"That's not Joslyn's parents." Henry says.

"Is this the people that told you they were Joslyn's parents Mr. Tate the colonel asks?"

"Yes. Yes it is."

"You mean that's not Joslyn's parents?" Dad says?

"No way." Henry says.

"That's all I needed to know." The colonel says and turns around and starts to leave.

"Oh yea. We believe these two and the other four that we are holding are the ones that kidnapped your daughter and was getting ready to smuggle her out of the country. Of course we can't be sure since we can't find your daughter, who would be able to identify them, because you people think this is some kind of game. These people aren't playing. If they find your kids before we do, then you will never see your kids again. You should really think about that the colonel says and walks off."

"It's not like we don't think of that ever-minute." Henry says.

"We really need to talk to the sheriff and see where there at."

"If he tells you, are you going to tell the colonel?" Dad asks.

"I don't know. I just know I would rather live with Shane hidden away on some military base than have him kidnapped by some foreign group and never see him again."

"I agree with you there. But I still don't think that's the right thing to do." Dad says.

"Well let's figure out a way to talk to the sheriff." Henry says.

A voice comes ringing down the hall as one of their keepers tells them to get back into their rooms.

"We'll talk about this later." Henry says as he starts walking toward his room.

"We may have a problem." Dad says as he walks back into the room.

"What's up?" Mom says.

"Well I think Henry is ready to tell the colonel where the girls are."

"Why?" Erica says.

"Well I think the colonel just played a major mind game on him, well actually on both of us."

"What happened?" Mom asks,

"Well you know Joslyn's parents that came by the house and we were trying to work with over at the Bevil's when Abby and Molly vanished?"

"Yes so?" Mom says.

"Turns out they aren't really Joslyn's parents they are with the Chinese people that grabbed the girls."

"What! That's not possible."

"The colonel has them here and just had me verify that they were the ones claiming to be Joslyn's parent and had Henry verify that they were not Joslyn's parents."

"Oh my God I can't believe this."

"The colonel used the opportunity to put pressure on us. Telling us that these were the people that grabbed Abby and Molly and they aren't playing games like us and if someone else grabs them we will never see them again."

"Well, he's right." Mom says.

"I know he's right, and now that the sheriff is in here who is taking care of them and protecting them out there? We have to figure out a way to talk to the sheriff." Dad says.

"I have a feeling they are going to open his door, like they have ours, and let us talk to him hoping he will tell us where they are. They will either be listening in or they figure as soon as we learn where they are we will tell them." Mom says.

"You know, I bet your right." Dad says.

As they are talking Debra walks in with a writing tablet and a couple pencils and puts them on the table.

"Here is the writing tablet and pencils that you asked for." She holds her finger up to her lip letting them know not to say anything about not asking for them.

"Oh thanks." Dad says.

"I really need to start writing things down because I can't remember stuff." Mom says.

Debra turns and walks out of the room. Mom takes a pencil and writes down on the tablet "I guess this means that they are listening to us". Dad shakes his head in agreement.

Henry and Joslyn walk into the room. Mom quickly writes on the tablet that they are listening to what they say and holds it up for them to read. They both shake their heads in acknowledgment.

"So, how are you guys doing today?" Henry asks.

"I'm bored and want to go home." Harlan says.

"Me to." Erica says.

"Well maybe they won't keep us here much longer." Joslyn says.

"Well I think if we can get the sheriff to tell us where the kids are, and we relay that to the colonel, we will at least get them out here with us." Henry says.

As Henry says that he points up to the ceiling with a finger and shakes his head no to let them know that he is only saying this to get the colonel to believe that they are ready to talk and maybe he will let the sheriff come in and talk to them.

CHAPTER TWENTY-TWO

WHO YOU GONNA CALL

No one could sleep and everyone stayed wide-awake thinking about what they were going to do first thing in the morning. Then the sweet smell of bacon sizzling in the pan came drifting through the bedroom and everyone jumped up and started getting ready. No alarm clock needed this morning. Everyone gathered at the kitchen table and Donna started dishing out breakfast.

"You guys make sure you get plenty to eat because this may be the only meal we get for a while." Donna says.

After everyone has their plates full she walks over to the radio and picks up the mic.

"Deputy Murphy you copy?"

"Go ahead this is Murphy."

"Deputy Murphy this is the sheriff's wife and I have a message from him, for you. Copy?"

"Roger that." The deputy says.

"Deputy Murphy the sheriff has been detained this morning and he needs you to go ahead with the plans that you and him discussed before, over." Donna says.

"Roger that Mrs. Hardery is everything ok over?"

"I will explain things to you later today over."

"Roger that, I will check in at 7:00 am, that is exactly forty five minutes from now over."

"Roger that." Donna says.

"Ok we have forty-five minutes and it will take twenty to get there so we have twenty-five minutes to get ready. I need to know exactly what we are going to do when we get there." Donna says.

"Just so we are all on the same page and no one is getting in the way of the other person, let me lay it out." I said.

"Donna, I think you should stay in the car and be ready to get out of there. We will go into the house first and go into my room. There should be a stack of CD's setting next to my computer. We want to get the one that has Lindsey Stirling written on it. From there we need to go out to the hay barn. In the back of the barn is an old water trough that hasn't been used in years; the Laptop is in the bottom of it. After we get it, I want to take a quick look around and make sure the dogs and the horses are all ok." I said.

"That's fine but don't take too long we have a very limited time to get this stuff." Donna says.

"Ok, if everyone is ready let's get in the car. We are going to take the sheriffs car so no one will mess with us." Donna says. She then pulls her hair back and puts it up under a cowboy hat. "It want hurt to look a little like the sheriff, right?"

"Works for me." I said.

"Ok go out to the garage and get down in the back seat. I need to start the generator so I can open the garage door. I'm going to leave it running just in case we have to pull in and hide real quickly." Donna says.

"Wow you're good at this." Shane says.

"I watch a lot of C.S.I." Donna says.

We head for the garage and get into the car. Donna raises the garage door and she backs out. She heads toward my house.

"Ok guys I'm going to go all the way around and come up by the Bevil's house. We will set there and wait for the all clear from Murphy."

As they go by the Bevil's house she can see that there is no one there so she pulls off the road and stops. After fifteen of the longest minutes, Murphy comes over the radio saying the road is clear.

"Roger that." Donna replies and she takes off.

She pulls down beside my house and all the way around to the hay barn.

"Ok guys it's show time so hurry up."

We all jump out of the car and head into the house. The back door is locked and I fumble around in the flowerpot until I find the key hidden there. I unlock the door and we run in. We run up the stairs and into my room.

"It's gone!" I yell out.

"What?" Molly asks.

"All of it. Look, the computer, the printer, the monitor, and all my CD's. They're all gone."

"Ok just chill a little. I'm sure the colonel had it all brought down to him just like he did mine. If he did then you'll get it all back one of these days." Shane says.

"Yea sure I will. Ok let's head to the barn." I said.

They run down the stairs and back outside. I carefully lock the back door and re-hide the key. Then we take off to the barn. I lead the way and we run to the back of the barn. We all stop at the same time.

"Oh my God! They filled the water trough with water. Why would they do that?" I said.

Shane rolls up his sleeve and sticks his hand down in the water. After feeling around from one end to the other he says, "Got it" and pulls the laptop up out of the water. As water pours out of it he says, "I think we can safely say that this laptop is never going to work again."

"I can't believe they did that. Why would they do that?" I said.

"Doesn't matter now, let's get out of here. You have to check on the dogs." Molly says.

I run around to the side of the house and the dogs start going nuts. I open the door to their pen and walk in. They jump all over me and I finally get down on my knees and just let them go crazy. Shane looks at their water and food.

"They have plenty of water and food. It looks like they are taking good care of them." Shane says.

I try to squeeze out the door without the dogs following me. Once I get out I Shane closes the door.

"Ok let's check the horses." I said.

We all run around to the horse barn and Molly slides open the door.

"Oh my God where are they?" I said.

All the horses, saddles, blankets, and bridles are gone.

"Where are they?" I yell.

"I don't know." Shane says.

"Surely the colonel didn't have them hauled off. What good would they be to him?" Molly says.

"I imagine that since there is no one here at night to watch the place, someone stole them." I said.

We hear Donna honk the car horn and so we take off running to the car.

As we get in the car Donna is yelling at us to get down.

"Murphy has the colonel stopped at the beginning of the road and he won't be able to hold him long."

Donna leaves my house like a professional racecar driver. When she hits the road she turns on the red lights and hollers for us to hang on.

"We are going out the back way and I hope he doesn't see us leaving."

After sliding sideways around a couple of corners she hits the main road and the race is on. The twenty-minute drive back to the house only took eight. She opens the garage door remotely and literally slides into the garage. She lets the door down.

"You guys open the cellar door and get ready to go down there in case someone followed us."

Donna walks into the living room and watches out the front window waiting to see if anyone followed them. After about ten minutes she yells for us to get in the cellar. Deputy Murphy pulls into the driveway and gets out of his car. He starts walking toward the house when the colonel's Humvee pulls in behind his car blocking the exit. The colonel and two soldiers get out of his vehicle and walk up to the deputy. The deputy turns and puts his hands on the hood of his car.

"Oh crap. It looks like they are arresting deputy Murphy." Donna says.

The colonel is walking this way so you guys be quiet down there. The colonel walks to the front door of the house and lets himself in.

"Excuse me! You can't just walk into my house!" Donna yells.

"So who you going to call, the sheriff's department? Your congressman? What were you doing out at the Tate's place this morning Mrs. Hardery?" The colonel asks.

"I was doing my husband's job, since he can't, because you have him locked up somewhere."

"Your husband's job, and what would that be Mrs. Hardery?"

"To make sure the house is locked up and the animals are taken care of since you have the Tates locked up somewhere also." Donna says.

"So was everything ok out there?" The colonel asks.

"No. Everything is not ok out there. All the horses are gone along with all the riding equipment. Did you have it locked up to?" Donna asks.

"No I didn't. You might not have heard, but the country is in a real crisis and people can't buy fuel for their cars so they steal other people's horses and riding equipment so they can get around and look for stuff like food, medicine, and water. Things like that."

"So you're saying that since you locked up the Tate's and they aren't able to protect their property that anyone can come in and take what they want." Donna says.

"No, what I'm saying is, the Tate's don't want to play ball and tell me where their kids are so I'm not going to go out of my way to protect their property." The colonel says.

"Wow, it gives me such a warm feeling knowing that a fine upstanding colonel like yourself has been given the task of protecting the American people from its enemies."

"So Mrs. Hardery what role did this deputy play in your little operation this morning?" The colonel asks.

"He was the lookout. Making sure no undesirable types could trap me down at the Tate's barn." Donna says.

"So why don't you feel that the Bevil's deserve the same consideration. Why didn't you check out their place?" The colonel asks.

"Oh I was going to but I was interrupted by some of those undesirables I was talking about and so I had to leave." Donna says.

The colonel walks up to Donna and gets right up in her face.

"Mrs. Hardery I'm going to tell you the same thing I told you husband yesterday. You think this is all fun and games but these people are playing for keeps. When your three little friends end up dead don't come crying to me."

With that the colonel walks out the front door. He yells at the two soldiers and they release deputy Murphy and get in the Humvee with the colonel. Donna turns and speaks toward the utility room.

"You guys stay put the deputy is coming in now, and oh my God, I can't believe I just said all that to a colonel. I'm going to throw up."

Donna opens the front door and the deputy walks in.

"You ok Donna?"

"Yes I'm fine."

Donna puts her hand over her mouth and runs to the restroom. In a couple of minutes she walks back out.

"Sorry about that." Donna says.

"You sure you are ok?" The deputy asks again.

"Yes I'm fine."

"Would you please tell me what's going on?" The deputy asks.

"I think being spread eagle on the front of my own car gives me the right to know what's going on,"

"Do you trust the sheriff?" Donna asks.

"With my life." The deputy replies.

"Then trust him in this. Remember he told you that the less you know the better off you would be." Donna says.

"Right. He said that."

"Then trust him and believe me, you don't want to know what's going on."

"Ok, can you tell me where the sheriff is?"

"Yes. He has been taken into custody by the colonel and as far as I can tell he is being held out at the ranch." Donna says.

"The sheriff has been arrested?" The deputy asks.

"Yes he has. And his departing words were for us to get done those things we were supposed to do."

"Ok, how can I help?"

"Just take care of the normal sheriff stuff while he's locked up. Keep an eye on the colonel and his men and keep a watchful eye on this place. Make sure the bad guys don't get into this house."

"Ok." The deputy says.

"Also, I may be taking a short trip to Oklahoma City tomorrow and I want you to make sure the colonel and his men don't follow me. And one other thing, do you know if that Andy Records guy is still out at his old place Donna asks?"

"Yes he's still there. It will take more than a world crisis to get that weirdo out of his home." The deputy says.

"Great. I'm going to run out to his place in a couple of hours."

"Do you want me to go with you?" The deputy asks.

"No, I want you to park in the front yard and keep an eye on this place. Don't let anyone in or out. I don't want the colonel's men ransacking the place while I'm gone."

"Ok, consider it done." The deputy says.

"I'll call you when I'm ready to leave."

"Great I'll be waiting for your call."

With that the deputy walks out to his car and leaves.

CHAPTER TWENTY-THREE

SHOTS FIRED

"You guys can come up now." Donna says to the empty utility room.

Once again they come up from the cellar and I slide the clothes hamper back into place.

"That's so cool. It makes me think we are in some kind of spy movie or something." I said.

"No, actually I think we are in some kind of real spy movie." Molly says.

As we walk into the kitchen Donna drops into one of the chairs at the table.

"I can't believe I just did that." Donna says.

"Me neither." I said.

"Ok, well I'll go by myself out to this Andy guys place and see if he is interested in helping us out." Donna says.

"Only I'm not going to say us, and Shane you need to make me understand what I need to ask him."

"Just ask him if he would be interested in sending an antivirus to the Space Station and the rover to be re-transmitted around the world. He will definitely be interested in that but when he asks if the colonel is on board with it, he may change his mind. You have to be very vague on what it actually is and how it all works." Shane says.

"Oh I will definitely be vague because I don't have a clue about half the stuff you are talking about." Donna says.

"You also have to figure he may try to set us up. The colonel may set up some sort of trap that he will spring while we are there."

"I think it's just better all-around if we go up to Eric's place and do it from there." I said.

"I think you're probably right, but he lives on the west side of Oklahoma City and we will have to drive right through town to get there and I don't think it's safe." Donna says.

"Mrs. Hardery this is deputy Murphy over," comes crackling over the radio.

"Go ahead this is she, over."

"I know you were planning on leaving your house and going out to visit someone but please be advised that we have a large number of people roaming around town that appear to have been staying at the F.E.M.A. Camp. It is my understanding that the camp out there has been set on fire and these people are now in town and they are very angry, over."

"Roger that deputy I will take that under advisement, over."

"If you would like for me to escort you I would be more than happy to."

"Roger that. As a matter of fact come by here and pick me up and we will go there together over."

"Roger that. I'm headed your way."

"You guys just stay out of sight and when he pulls up I will walk out and get in his car. Just remember we will be coming back in thirty to forty five minutes and make sure he can't see you when he pulls up and drops me off." Donna says.

"Ok tell me what you're going to tell him." Shane says to Donna.

"Ok, I have heard of someone who has an antivirus for the Monarch Virus. This person has figured out a way to broadcast this antivirus to the world through the Mars Rover and they need to use your equipment to do it. Will you help them?" Donna says.

"Yes, I would love to help them. Is colonel Krom on board with this?"

"No."

"Why not?"

"Because they feel that the fewer people involved the better the chances of success."

"Wow <u>you</u> good." I said.

"That was a good answer Donna. I think you're ready." Shane says.

"There is only one problem with all this." I said.

"What?" They all say in unison.

"We don't have the antivirus remember. The CD's were gone, the laptop destroyed, we don't have the antivirus." I reiterate.

"That's true." Molly says.

"Yes we do." Shane says.

"It's right there on your arm." He points to my iPod.

"Do you really think you can get it off here?" I ask Shane.

"There is about a one in a thousand chance we can. But that's the only chance we have right now." Shane says.

"Well maybe Donna should hold off on going out to Andy's until we get the thing off my iPod." I said.

"No. We can't wait any longer; it's only getting worse out there." Donna says.

"Andy has probably got the right equipment out there to pull the cocoon off the iPod if it is even possible." Shane says.

"Ok then let's give it a shot." Donna says.

"The deputy just pulled up." Molly says.

"Ok you guys stay out of sight." Donna says.

"We will. Good luck." I said.

Donna heads out to the car.

"You know I'm kind off wishing we had the protection that the ranch has to offer right now." I said.

"So does either one of you know how to cook or make coffee?" Shane asks.

"I know how to cook but I'm not going to just start opening drawers and going through things," I said.

"Why not?" Shane asks.

"This isn't my house that's why." I said.

"You know she don't care if you fix something." Shane says.

"No. She will be back in thirty minutes and you can ask her to fix something. You're not going to starve to death in thirty minutes." I said.

"Ok, while you guys argue about ethics or protocol or whatever you call it I'm going to make some coffee." Molly says.

"I didn't say we couldn't make coffee. That's totally different. She won't care if we do that." I said.

So Molly looks around and finds the ingredients to make coffee and starts making some. She also gets the milk and juice out of the refrigerator and sets them on the table.

"For those of us who realize that we are only twelve years old and shouldn't be drinking coffee we can drink milk or juice." Molly says.

"Wait a minute, your making coffee and you don't even drink coffee?" I ask.

"Ooh no, I think it's disgusting." Molly replies.

"Then why are you making it?" I ask.

"Because Shane wants some." Molly says.

"Shane can make his own coffee if Shane wants coffee." I said.

"Wow, someone got up on the wrong side of the bed this morning." Molly says.

"I'm just joking." I said. "I would be more than happy to serve you coffee Mr. Bevil."

I get a cup out of the cabinet and set it in front of Shane then I ask him if he would like cream and sugar.

"Yes ma'am." Shane replies.

"Ma'am. Did you just call me ma'am?" I ask.

"No ma'am I didn't," Shane replies.

We all start laughing and then Molly and I set down and join Shane but we drink juice. After about twenty minutes Molly gets up and looks out the window.

"Guys. We have company." Molly says.

Shane and I walk over to where Molly is watching out the front window. Two dark brown cars have pulled up in front of the house. One slowly rolls down the drive way and the other one parks in a position to block the street.

"Is the front door locked?" I ask.

Molly takes her hand and slowly turns the dead bolt on the front door.

"It is now." Molly says.

Two men, that appear to be of Middle Eastern decent, get out of the first car in the drive way and head toward the back of the house. The other two head toward the front of the house.

"We have to get in the cellar." I said.

We almost fall over each other as we run to the utility room and pull back the clothes hamper. I run back into the kitchen and grab the microphone to the radio and with a very deep voice say, "Help the sheriffs house is being robbed, please help the sheriff's house is being robbed."

Then I run back into the utility room and we head down to the cellar making sure that the clothes hamper is back in place. We set very quietly and listen to the speaker. We hear the sound of glass breaking and then the sound of footsteps walking around above us. We hear an occasional crashing sound as the men are tossing things around as they look around the house. We very faintly hear what appears to be vehicles pulling into the front yard and a siren, that is way off in the distance, is getting closer fast. The men in the house appear to start running around in the house and then we hear the back door slam twice. There is a moment of silence then we can hear the men yelling to each other in a language that neither of us understand. There was another short period of silence and then gunshots started ringing out. About eight shots are heard then it is quiet again. The siren has now made it to the front yard and abruptly goes silent.

The very distinguishable voice of the colonel is heard telling someone to get an ambulance in here for those guys and take the other two out to the ranch. The next voice we hear is that of Donna as she runs into the house.

"What happened? Who are those men?" Donna yells.

"Calm down Mrs. Hardery everything is under control." The colonel says. "They are just a few of the nice people that want those kids that you are hiding. They were obviously monitoring the sheriff's radio just like we were and since you made it clear that the deputy was coming by and picking you up, they probably felt it was a good time to come by and see if the kids were here or if there was anything lying around that might tell them where they are. Surely after this you are ready to hand them over to me."

"I can't hand over something I don't have." Donna says.

The deputy runs into the house and starts checking things out and then asks Donna if everything is ok.

"Yes everything is ok. Looks like I have a mess to clean up and a window to replace, but everything else seems ok."

An ambulance pulls into yard and pulls to the back. The paramedics get out to load the two guys into the ambulance when one of the soldiers says to him, "There is no hurry they didn't make it. Just load them up and take them to the morgue".

The soldiers help the paramedics load the two bodies into the ambulance. The paramedics get into the ambulance, turn off the emergency lights and drive away.

Two other soldiers come from the back rooms of the house and tell the colonel it is all clear back there.

"Thanks guys." Donna says as they walk out of the house.

"So we have an interesting problem here Mrs. Hardery." The colonel says.

"What's that?" Donna replies.

"Well, we have what were obviously some Middle Eastern gentlemen, who I would be willing to bet are in this country illegally, breaking into your house. That's going to require a lot of paper work explaining how all this went down. The real problem is the part of the report that deals with how we were tipped off that this was going down. I will need to fill that out along with the rest of it. So you got any ideal who might have made that call over the radio telling us the house was being robbed."

"I don't know who it was but when you figure out who it was please let me know so I can thank them." Donna says.

"You know it sounded kind of like a young girl trying to fake a deep voice to me." The colonel says.

"Really. Why would some young girl not want to be recognized when doing something as great as stopping a burglary?" Donna says with a quizzical look on her face.

"Look Hardery, I know there here somewhere in the neighborhood, or across the street, or hiding up in a tree and I will find them. And when I do you and your husband both are going to rot in prison."

Deputy Murphy steps up and says, "I think your done here colonel. This is a crime scene in my jurisdiction and unless you have something more to add to this investigation I think it's time you left."

The colonel turns and walks out.

CHAPTER TWENTY-FOUR

GARTH BROOKS BOULEVARD

"Well as you expected Andy is not going to help us unless the colonel is in on it. He was really amazed that I the sheriff's wife thought she had an antivirus that would get the country out of this mess. He even asks if I had a copy with me." Donna says.

"I don't think he believed me at first, but he did say that using the rover was a great way to get it out to the world. He was also really curious as to how we were going to let the world know. So I didn't tell him about that part just in case he turned on us.

He couldn't understand why the government hadn't been given a copy of it and then of course <u>they</u> could up it to the rover or a few hundred satellites or systems. When I told him they didn't want the world to have this they wanted to keep it to for themselves and use it as a weapon. He said that would be even better. I really got the impression that he was going to call the colonel right then, but we got your call about the house being robbed and had to leave. I did tell him that this was very confidential information and unless he wanted the colonel coming down on him he had better keep quiet about it. That seem to puzzle him but at the same time he said ok. Hey it was worth a shot."

"So our only other shot is Eric Hill." Shane says.

"That's true, but you need to understand that driving up there is borderline insane. The deputy told me about some of the things that are happening up there and it's going to be tough.

So if we are going to do that then we need to leave right now. If Andy called the colonel he is going to be all over us real quick." Donna says.

"Then let's get out of here." I said.

"We better eat something first because it might be a while before we get back and there is nothing to eat on the road." Shane says.

"Right, Shane is starving to death and wanted me to fix something but I said no."

"Wow if you had of we could get out of here now." Donna says.

"Ouch." Shane says as he pokes me with his finger.

"How about if I just grab some sandwich stuff and we take it with us?" Donna says.

"Sounds good to me." I said.

"Grab some bottles of water and let's load up."

We all go into the garage and get into the car. Donna brings a paper sack with foodstuff in it and Shane has the bottled water. I get in the front and Shane and Molly get in the back.

"You guys need to lie down and stay down until we get out of town. I'm going to pull out then run into the house and kill the generator. No need it running all day. Ready?"

Donna backs the car out and lets the garage door down. She gets out of the car and runs into the house and then comes running back. She fumbles with the key trying to get it back in the ignition and ends up dropping them on the floorboard. She finally gets them in the ignition and gets the car started.

"I'm sorry guys. I never said I would be a good get-a-way car driver. Here we go."

Donna backs the car out into the street and starts down the road. She looks in the rear view mirror and sees the colonels Humvee coming up behind them.

"Oh crap."

"What is it?" I ask.

"The colonel just stopped in front of the house and it looks like he may have seen us because he appears to be coming after us."

Donna speeds up and is driving about twice the speed limit. She comes to a road and makes a sliding turn to the left. She puts the pedal to the metal and is driving like a crazy woman. She sees the deputy's car pull onto the road behind her.

"Great, the deputy's car and this one looks almost identical maybe the colonel will think that he is us and stop him." Donna says as she takes a hard right turn to get out of site.

She drives through a large dip in the road and we all fly up in the air and then come crashing down again.

"Wow when you said this trip was going to be dangerous I thought you meant when we got to Oklahoma City not a mile from the house." I said.

"Ok guys we are almost out of town. We are getting on thirty-five right now so you can get up and help me watch behind to see if we are being followed.

So the sheriff left us a full tank of gas and it's only about sixty-five miles so we should be good on fuel. Of course the sheriff thought he was going to be using the gas himself as he drove us there but things change.

Ok we stay on thirty-five south until we hit the city and then we go west on sixty six until we get to Yukon which is where his place is. Of course we don't know where his place is in Yukon and if we blink we will totally miss it so we will just worry about that when we get there. I'm sorry I just talk a lot when I'm nervous." Donna says.

"Boy, you do talk a lot when you're nervous." Molly says.

"Yes I do. Way too much. All the time. Deputy Murphy said we might not be able to get on sixty-six. He said there were a lot of cars setting all over the road. Some of them have been burned. Some of them wrecked. He said if it's blocked off the best bet would be to go all the way in to town and get on Interstate forty. He said they were trying to keep it open but there were a lot of groups of people walking down it and they are looting and taking anything they can get especially if it has gasoline in it and is driving down the road. I think that since we are in a police car they will leave us alone. Ok I'm going to shut up now."

About thirty minutes pass by.

"Well this is Guthrie so we are half way there." I said.

"Whoa look at all the cars on the road. Make sure your doors are locked and cover up the food or anything else that they might want to try and get." Donna says.

"I think we should turn around and go back. At least the cellar is safe." Molly says.

"Well let's keep going. If it starts getting bad we will turn around and go back. We are not going to be able to go over about ten miles an hour with me having to weave in and out of these parked cars. Oh crap. There's a man standing in the middle of the road and it looks like he has a big pipe in his hand. Ya'll hold on because I'm not stopping." Donna says.

"You can't just run over him." I said.

"He'll move. It's time to put on the hat." Donna says.

She tucks her hair under the cowboy hat and then reaches over and turns the red lights on. When she gets up to the guy she blast a short burst on the siren. The man jumps back out of the way.

"Whoa that was awesome." I said.

"You didn't see that one on CSI." Molly says.

"I thought for sure I was going to have to hit him." Donna says. "Ok it looks clear for a little while. I'm going to speed up as fast as I can. There are no more little towns like that until we get to Edmond and then just passed that is where we hit sixty-six."

"Shane can you hand me a bottle of water please?" I ask.

"Go easy on the water unless you want to get out and pee on the side of the road with all these people." Donna says.

"Are you ok Shane?" I ask.

"I'm fine." Shane replies.

"You sure are quiet."

"I'm fine. How am I supposed to hand you a bottle of water when there is a steel mesh partition between us?"

"Just roll down your window and hand it to me around the outside."

"Uh, there's no window roller thing or door-opening thing." Shane says.

"Yep, it's a sheriff's car, the sheriff doesn't like the bad guys chocking him while he's driving, or opening the door and jumping out, or crawling out the window." Donna says.

"So I guess I'll wait on that water until we stop." I said.

"Do we have any way to find Eric when we get there? I mean, I'm not sure we should be pulling up to people on the side of the road and asking directions." Molly says.

"All I remember is there were a few large antennas that you could see from the road. Oh yea, the name of the road he lives on is Garth Brooks Boulevard." Shane says.

"Garth Brooks Boulevard are you kidding me?" I said.

"How cool is that?" Molly says. "Yea I live on Garth Brooks Boulevard."

"His parent's house is sitting on the top of a hill and it is surrounded by a lot of pastureland. Eric has his equipment in these three converted tornado shelters and it's kind of like a bunker because it is mostly underground. As a matter of fact that's what his mom calls it. His bunker. Anyway when we get close we should be able to see the antenna towers."

"If Eric lives on the hill then he's not friends with Garth, because all Garth's friends live in low places." Molly says as she cracks up laughing. "Come on, you have to admit that was funny."

"I'm just totally amazed that you know some of the lyrics to a Garth Brooks song." Donna says.

"I know the whole song; do you want me to sing it?" Molly asks?

"No thanks were good." I said.

"All right we are at Edmond look for the sixty-six turn off." Donna says.

"Would that be it up there with all the barricades in front of it?" I ask.

"Wonderful. I was afraid of that. That means we have to go all the way into town and get on interstate forty. Look in the glove compartment and see if there's a map in there." Donna says.

I open the glove compartment and remove an Oklahoma City map. I open it up and try to figure out where we are.

"Just when you need your iPad for directions somebody goes and blows up the Internet so you can't use it." I said.

"That's not funny." Shane says.

"I'm sorry. I keep forgetting that that <u>somebody</u> is you." I said.

"I wish I could forget." Shane says.

I show Donna where we are on the map.

"Ok we are here and we need to be here. Wow we sure have a lot of City to go through. If they have sixty-six blocked off I hate to see what it's going to be like when we get close to downtown. It looks like Interstate thirty-five runs right into forty so if we just stay on this we will run right into it. Then it's a long way around interstate forty to Garth Brooks Blvd. We cross the Will Rogers Expressway and then the John Kilpatrick Turnpike and then we hit Garth." I said.

"Have you guys noticed that there is absolutely no traffic on this road?" Donna asks.

"It's really creepy." Molly says.

"If you look down at the side roads and streets off in the distance there is no traffic. A lot of cars but none of them are moving. The deputy said that there were a lot of people out in the streets but I'm not seeing any." Donna says.

"Well just look up the road in front of us there are plenty of them up ahead." I said.

CHAPTER TWENTY-FIVE

THE COLONEL'S TRUE COLORS

The colonel comes busting into the room without knocking or announcing himself. Dad jumps up and says, "Excuse me." The colonel tells him to set down.

"I've played around with you people all I'm going to. It's time we start talking and I mean now."

No one says anything. The colonel yells out to Debra.

"I want you to bring the sheriff, the Bevil's, and the Tanton's in here right now."

The colonel is visibly angry and has some papers rolled up in his hand and he is beating on the table with them. Debra runs to get everyone as fast as she can. In a few minutes the Bevil's and the Tanton's walk into the room.

"So what's going on?" Henry asks.

"I think the colonel has something he wants to tell us." Dad says.

Debra escorts the sheriff in and closes the door behind him.

"Ok people, I wanted to get you all together so that you could all hear what I have to say. All at the same time. I don't

182

want anyone having to depend on hearsay or second hand information. I want to make sure each and every one of you know I said what I said.

Now. I really can't understand what kind of philosophy, or code of honor, or religion, that people like you subscribe to. I don't understand what would make you put the lives of your loved ones in jeopardy, to actually put them in harm's way, just to keep your country from learning information from them that would not only strengthen your countries defenses but stop some other country that wants to do us harm from getting hold of that information.

How has the country, that has given you everything, that you claim to love, how has it became the evil empire?"

"It's not our country, it's you." Dad says.

"Me." The colonel says.

"How am I the bad guy when all I've done is try to protect your kids?"

"You're not trying to protect the kids or their parents from anything other than somebody else getting to them first and getting the code for this virus." The sheriff says.

"You don't care that these kids are going to be locked away somewhere for years, denied a normal childhood, yanked out of their schools, and away from their relatives as long as you get your code." Angela says.

"I want deny that." The colonel says.

"I think that them being taken care of for what might be years by their government is a small price to pay to keep something this powerful out of the hands of some foreign country." The colonel says.

"And into the hands of our government." The sheriff says.

"Exactly. Do you know how many lives could be saved if we could take down a countries infrastructure, their ability to communicate and launch attacks?"

"None." Henry says.

"Are you crazy? It would save thousands of lives on both sides." The colonel says.

"How many people died during World War Two? They didn't have the Internet or computers then." Henry says.

"But things are different now." The colonel says.

"We have the Internet. We have computers and so do they. Warfare is now electronic the country who has the best technology has the greatest edge in a war now." The colonel says.

"This week. Next week that might not be the case. Things have a habit of changing rather quickly now days." The sheriff says.

"That's crazy." The colonel says. "Do you really think things are going to change and the world is going to go back to the way it was before we had computers?"

"It just did." Harlan says.

"Wow! Out of the mouth of babes." The sheriff says.

"One twelve year old boy just took us back into the stone ages so to speak and your trying to tell us that we as a country are going to rely on something as fragile as the network infrastructure and the Internet. I think this should be a wakeup call to the whole world that we have become too dependent on computers. That we need to take a look at how we live and figure out a better way to exist and carry on the day-to-day business of eating and drinking." Dad says.

"I guarantee that these foreign countries you keep referring to have their best people working day and night trying to come up with a way to defend themselves from such an attack, and I'm sure they have some twelve year old kids over there that can figure it out." Angela says.

"You can set back and dream of your better way and how things ought to be but that doesn't change the fact that the country that you call home needs this information to better protect itself. It also needs to make sure that our enemies don't end up with it enabling them to do us harm. That information is in the mind of your son and I want to know where he is.

If I don't know where he is by noon tomorrow I'm going to have all of you adults transferred to a military prison in

Leavenworth Kansas where you will be held without bail until you can be tried for treason. The two juveniles will be placed in the custody of a federal Marshal until a suitable foster home can be found. Do I make myself clear?"

"You can't prosecute them for not telling you something they don't know." The sheriff says.

"Watch me!" The colonel snaps back.

He starts to walk out and turns around and walks back to the table. He takes the papers he had been holding and throws them down on the table. With the papers are two eight by ten pictures.

"Oh yea, here is something else you might want to consider tonight, why you're thinking about this. Those pictures are of the two North Korean soldiers we shot and killed while they were trying to get into your house sheriff. Maybe they didn't get the message that one of their twelve years olds back home was figuring out a way to solve their problem."

"Comments like that is why we think you're the bad guy colonel, and it's really not that we think you're a bad guy, we really think you're a jerk." Joslyn says.

"Corporal Penson stand guard in here and watch the sheriff and others until they are ready to return to their rooms." The colonel turns and walks out.

"Ok everyone, remember, they can hear everything we say in here." Dad says.

Erica looks at the pictures on the table and says, "Oh my god; they shot this guy right between the eyes."

"I want to see!" Harlan yells as he runs over to Erica.

"No! You don't need to be looking at those either Erica." Mom says.

Mom grabs them away from Erica and looks at them herself.

"So sheriff, are our kids ok?" Angela asks.

The sheriff shakes his head in the affirmative but says, "I really don't know Mrs. Tate. I wish I did".

"What are we going to do? We don't know where the kids are but the colonel is going to haul us off to Leavenworth and have us locked up." Henry asks.

The sheriff walks over to the table and picks up a pencil and a piece of paper. He writes on it <u>your kids are with my wife and are fine</u>. Joslyn grabs the sheriff and hugs him.

"So what do you think we should do sheriff?" Angela asks.

"Well, there is not much we can do really. We don't know where they are so we can't tell him anything and he is going to do what he's going to do."

"I think it's time for them to come out here." Angela says.

"I think we should tell the colonel everything we know and let him pick them up."

"Well, once again, what can we tell him?" Henry says.

"Remember, even if they are brought out here and Shane tells them what they want to know, you still won't get to go home. You're going to be held in protective custody until Shane's knowledge is no longer an asset or a risk. The only way that can change or be fixed, if you will, is if the code for the virus as well as an antivirus be given to everybody that wants a copy. Every country, every military, everybody. Then it's not a threat to anyone and then Shane will no longer be of value to our government or anybody else." The sheriff says.

"Yea but how could that ever happen?" Dad asks?

"Well I don't know Shane that well but I bet he is trying to figure out a way to do that." The sheriff says.

As the sheriff is speaking he writes on the paper <u>He has a way figured out</u> and holds it up for everybody to see.

"But if he is locked up out here then any chance he has of making something like that happen will be over." The sheriff says.

"Yea but if he is captured by some other group then he will end up in a lot worse situation than he would be out here and wouldn't be able to do anything about it either." Henry says.

The sheriff writes on the paper, <u>We must stall the colonel for forty-eight hours. If Shane hasn't succeeded by then we tell</u>

the colonel where to find them and then he holds it up so they can read it. Dad takes the paper and writes <u>how do we stall them?</u> the sheriff writes <u>we wait until in the morning, that buys us twenty hours, then I will take them on a wild goose chase and try to buy some more.</u> The sheriff holds it up for everyone to see. Everyone shakes his or her head in agreement.

"So do you think those pictures are real, I mean do you really think they killed those two guys?" Erica asks.

"I think it's just the colonel trying to scare us. There is no telling where those pictures came from." Henry says.

"Yea but they could be real and if they are that means they were that close to getting Abby." Erica says.

"He said they were trying to break into my house, so you are thinking that she is at my house." The sheriff says.

"So if she's not there then where is she?" Erica asks.

Everyone looks at Erica with a what the heck are you doing look on their faces. Erica does a rolling motion with her hands telling them to go along with her. Everyone catches on to what she doing and joins in.

"Yea sheriff, obviously the North Koreans thought they were at you house or else they wouldn't have tried to break in." Joslyn says.

"The only reason they think that they are at my place, or that I know where they are, is because the colonel thinks that. He has his men following me around and he keeps coming over to my place, so sure they think I know." The sheriff says.

"Aren't you afraid for your wife, I mean she lives in the house they tried to break into?" Angela asks.

"Sure I am. But once again we don't know for sure if the pictures are even real."

The sheriff starts writing on the paper again. He motions for Debra to come over to where he is. He hands her the paper and she reads it and shakes her head in the affirmative. The sheriff very quietly destroys all the papers that they had written on.

"Well I'm going back to my room. I guess we wait and see what the colonel is going to do in the morning when he finds out we don't know where they are. Does anyone know how Shane escaped from here? I mean if the colonel is going to start shipping people to Leavenworth then I might try getting out of here myself." The sheriff asks.

The sheriff has a smile on his face and holds a thumb up to indicate he is just messing with those that are listening to them.

CHAPTER TWENTY-SIX

DEMOLITION DERBY

"Ok guys make sure you have your seat belts drawn tight. We may have to play demolition derby up here. I don't know that being in this sheriff's car is such a good idea. People tend to get very angry at authority types when they are in the middle of a crisis. You know they tend to blame those authority types for letting this happen." Donna says.

"Now you bring that up. Little late to break into psychology one-o-one here." I said.

About a quarter mile up the road the road is completely blocked off by stalled vehicles and people.

"Hang on." Donna says.

She heads the car into the median, bounces across it and starts driving the wrong way into oncoming traffic. Luckily there is no oncoming traffic. As soon as she passes the blockage she pulls back across the median and gets back into the right lane.

"Ok I see an area ahead that has no people and there is a space where there are no cars. I'm going to pull over and stop.

Abby, I want you to open your door and then open Shane's. Shane you hand her a few bottles of water and then Abby you close Shane's door and get back in as quickly as possible." Donna says.

"I'm not really that thirsty." I said.

"I am." Donna says.

"Really, we are pulling over to get a drink in the middle of a war zone." Molly says.

"Only one bottle is for drinking we will use the other if we get into a jam and have to buy our way out. I figure between this shotgun and a bottle of water most people will let us through for the water." Donna says.

"I'm really starting to wonder how you know all this stuff. I'm not buying the whole C.S.I. thing." I said.

"I spent two years with the Marines in Iraq and did the whole Desert Storm thing before the sheriff and I got married." Donna says.

"Really. I didn't know that." I said.

"That's super cool." Molly says.

"I was a sergeant and I specialized in MOUT."

"MOUT, what the heck is that?" Molly asks.

"It's Military Operations on Urbanized Terrain. Or in civilian terms it's sort of urban operations and control tactics. Yea I'm starting to have flash backs because this is what I had to deal with on a day-to-day basis over there." Donna says.

"So given the situation were in, we couldn't be with a better person." I said.

"I wouldn't say that." Donna says.

They pull off the road and I jump out. I open Shane's door and the transaction goes perfectly until I drop the water. I start trying to capture it as it rolls away.

"Hurry up Abby there is a pick-up coming this way." Donna says.

I throw the water I have into the front seat of the car and then head down the embankment to get the last bottle.

"Just leave it!" Donna yells.

I keep on until I grab the bottle. I climb back up the slope and get to the car just as the pick-up pulls up to the car on Donna's side. The pick-up has three people in front and three in back. The guy setting by the window rolls down the window just as I get back in the car.

"Is everything ok sheriff?" The guy asks.

"Yea were fine. Just had to take a break if you know what I mean." Donna replies.

"You're going to run into some really bad stuff about a mile and a half on down the road so I would suggest getting off on one of the side roads." The guy says.

"I appreciate the information." Donna says.

The truck takes off.

"I'm sorry. I don't juggle water bottles very well when I'm under pressure I guess." I said.

"Actually it turned out for the best. They gave us some important information that we wouldn't have found out if it weren't for you being a klutz." Donna says.

"Thanks, I need all the self-esteem boosters I can get right now." I said.

"Ok, let's roll." Donna says as she pulls back onto the road.

I open the map and look at where we are.

"If the problem is a mile and a half up the road then that places it right where we need to merge from thirty five into forty. Looks like there is a big mix master there and that's probably where the problem is." I said. "If you get off on West Reno Avenue we can take it all the way down to where it connects with forty again and get back on forty or go a little farther and turn on North Cemetery Road, which turns into Garth Brooks. Surely the trouble spot they are talking about won't reach that far."

"I think right now all of Oklahoma City is a trouble spot." Molly says.

"Ok, watch for a way to get on that Reno Street." Donna says.

"Are there any parks on that street?" Donna asks.

"I don't see any but if we went north a little we could hit one." I said.

"No, we need to avoid parks, baseball fields, things like that." Donna says.

"Why?" Molly asks.

"People tend to congregate in places like that when there is no other place to go. Plus, if the city has anything going on, you know, trying to help people out, they usually set up shop in those type places."

"There it is, exit here." I point ahead to the exit.

Donna heads down Reno Ave.

"Wow look around." I said.

"Every store has the windows broken out or their doors kicked in. How do people get like this?" Molly asks.

"It's because some twelve-year-old idiot destroyed their ability to function normally." Shane says.

"Not really. That may be the reason that sparked the feeling of hopelessness and despair, but that doesn't answer why some of the people sit quietly in their homes waiting for someone to fix things or they even go out of their homes and try to help fix the problem.

Then you have the second group, affected by the exact same situation, go berserk and feel that they have to destroy everything in a fit of rage.

The third group is the opportunist who sees the front door to an appliance store kicked in and takes that opportunity to upgrade their TV, computer, or sound system at no charge.

The forth group is those that have to feed their families and are hungry themselves. They might not do something bad or illegal to feed themselves but they will do <u>anything</u> to feed their kids."

Then you have what's called the mob mentality. When groups two, three, and four wind up in the same place at the same time and for some reason they figure it's time to pay back those people who are not fixing the problem, they band together and feel they are the majority and the majority is always right, so they destroy, loot, burn, kill, and take whatever they want.

I don't think anybody has ever come up with a good answer to why it's that way. Oh, look at that." Donna says.

"What?" I ask?

"That girl standing by herself on the side of the road can't be over four years old."

"Oh yea I see here. She is all by herself." Molly says.

"Pull over and see if we can do something." I said.

"As bad as I want to I'm afraid it might be a trap." Donna says.

"A trap?" I said.

"Someone may be using her as bait."

"As bait?" Molly says.

"Give me a break." Shane says.

"We have to stop for her." I said.

"Ok, then here's how we do this. Everybody make sure your doors are locked. I'm going to pull up by the girl. You open your door Abby and show her a bottle of water. If she comes toward you, grab her and pull her in. Then you close your door and lock it immediately. If she starts backing up when she sees the water, close your door and lock it immediately."

"Ok I don't understand the purpose for all that but let's do it." I said.

Donna reaches over and releases the latch that keeps the shotgun in its restraint.

"Whoa, do you really think we need that to pick up a four year old?" I ask.

"Just in case my hunch is right. Ok here we go." Donna says.

Donna pulls the car up in front of the little girl. I open the door and show her the water. The little girl backs up really quickly and Donna starts yelling "Close your door, close your door."

As I get the door closed there are about eight people coming in all different directions heading toward the car. Donna turns the wheel very sharply as she floorboards the car just as her window and Shane's window burst into a million pieces. As Donna spins the car around she runs over three of the men and the car bounces up violently as she drives over one of them.

"Oh my God! Oh my God! I start screaming hysterically.

"Just hang on!" Donna yells. They start to take off when one of the guys jumps on the hood. Donna starts making violent turns to the left and right as she builds up speed.

"This guy just won't let go!" Donna yells.

Then she slams on the breaks while making a sharp turn to the left. The guy goes flying off and rolling across the pavement. She then straightens up and takes off down Reno Street. She reaches over and turns on the emergence lights.

"Is everybody ok?" She asks.

"I'm fine." Molly says.

"Me to." Shane says.

"Other than being scarred for life, I'm fine." I said.

"Ok, we don't stop to pick up or assist anybody else right?" Donna says.

"Right," they all three reply.

"How much farther is it to this place?" Molly asks.

"Well that's the Will Rogers Turnpike we are coming up on so it looks like it's about eleven miles." I said.

"Shane, are you ok with the glass back their?" Donna asks?

"Yea, it just shattered. None of it has fallen out yet." Shane says.

"Cool." Donna says.

I start looking at the map again.

"We are not going back home this way. I'm going to figure out a way to go back on the farm roads." I said.

"Sounds good to me. Besides if the colonel has figured out where we went he will be coming down thirty five just like we did, and he will definitely be watching for us." Donna says.

"Wow, look over there that building is totally engulfed in flames." I said.

"I guess they don't have the water pumps up and running yet, so they don't have any way to put it out. Luckily we still have water towers that cover most of Perry." Shane says.

"Why does that make us lucky?" I ask.

"Because we don't depend on electric pumps for water pressure. Our water is stored in those big ugly tanks on top of the towers. Being up that high creates a lot of pressure. Water runs downhill so to speak, and so when it gets to the facet in your house it still has a lot of that pressure behind it. Here they store the water in large reservoirs and they are at the same level as the houses. They have to use pumps to get the water to the house and have enough pressure for you to take a shower."

"So our system is better." Molly says.

"I think so." Shane says.

"The only problem with our system is that we have to use pumps to pump the water up into the tower so when it runs out we can't refill it until we can get the pumps going again. However during a crisis situation they only allow the water to be used for emergences like fires and I believe the hospital is allowed to use it." Donna says. "Ok we just passed the John Kilpatrick Turnpike so how far are we?"

"North Cemetery Road should be about two miles up the road. When you get to it take a right. We go back under forty and it turns into Garth Brooks. His house should be about a mile pass forty."

"Yep, there's the Cemetery road and I'm taking a right." Donna says.

"Well I hope after all this he is home." Shane says.

"Yea that would suck if we went through all this and he's not there." Molly says.

"Well if he's not then we will just camp out there until he gets back." Donna says.

"Yea about a day then I'm kicking in his door and using the equipment." Shane says.

"We are now going under forty." I say.

"So everybody start looking for those antennas." Donna says.

"Wow, I sure hope this is where he lives." Shane says.

"You better hope this is where he lives or we are going to put you on the hood and see how long you can hold on." I said.

"Bingo! I see antennas." Molly says.

"Yea boy." I said.

"That's the place." Shane says.

Donna pulls the car in just as Eric is walking from the house to the bunker.

As they pull in Eric sees them and starts walking toward them. I get out of car and open Shane's door. Shane's says "Hey big guy, how you doing?"

"Oh my God, what the heck are you doing all the way out here Eric asks?"

Eric grabs Shane's hand and starts to shake it.

"These are my friends Abby and Molly."

We reach out and shake his hand.

"This is Donna our sheriff's wife and a person that is now not only my friend but my hero."

"Glad to meet you." Donna says.

"So why are you here, and what's up with the sheriffs car? What have you done now Shane?"

"Well I guess it's no secret, but I caused this whole Internet fiasco."

"You know when it completely stopped working, I thought of you."

"Nice, thanks." Shane says.

"Oh you're serious. Whaaaat?" Eric says

"I'll explain all about that later, but we really need your help fixing this mess and I'm afraid a very ticked off colonel, that wants to stop us, is not too far behind us. Maybe two or three hours maybe longer."

CHAPTER TWENTY-SEVEN

ARE THESE THE GOOD GUYS?

Once again the colonel comes barging into the room totally unannounced.

"Corporal Penson can you get the others and bring them in here?"

The corporal escorts the others into the room and closes the door.

"Well its thirteen hundred hours, that's an hour longer than I had given you to give me the information I want. So it's now or never the colonel says."

No one says anything. Then Henry speaks up.

"We can't tell you what we don't know."

"So I guess we go to Leavenworth." Dad says.

"You're really going to let you children be put in foster care to keep me from picking up your daughter Mrs. Tate?"

"Like Henry said, we can't tell you what we don't know."

"So sheriff. You going to stand there and tell me you don't know where there at?"

"If I knew where they are right now I would tell you."

"Your job as sheriff is to protect these people and you're going to allow their kids to be kidnapped or even killed.

See there is one thing you might not have considered. If they grab all three of them the two girls are of no real use to them. Since they have Shane they will probably just kill them, you know to make sure there is no one left to identify them. Or they could haul them back to their country and sell them." The colonel says.

"Ok that's enough. Ship us off to Leavenworth or whatever but we've heard enough of you, your ridiculous accusations, and your crap, especially in front of these to young people. I don't want them to think that our military is made up of people like you. So leave." The sheriff says.

"I come and go as I please. I say whatever I please. In front of whomever I please." The colonel says as he stands up to leave. "I'll be arranging for your transportation so make sure you're ready." The colonel walks out of the room.

"Well I guess we will be going to Leavenworth." Joslyn says.

The sheriff looks at Debra and she shakes her head no and mouths the words he's bluffing. The sheriff walks over to the table and makes a writing motion with his hands. Harlan goes over to his bed and gets the tablet and pencil and hands it to the sheriff.

"That's a pretty nice picture you've drawn there." The sheriff says.

"Thanks." Harlan says.

"That's a bomb being dropped on someone right?"

"North Korea." Harlan says.

The sheriff turns the page and rights down something and hands it to Debra. She takes the pencil and writes something down and hands it back to the sheriff.

"Ok I guess we just set around and wait for someone to load us in a vehicle and take us out of here." The sheriff says.

The sheriff writes something on the paper and shows it to everyone. It says that the kids are safe and that Homeland security should be arriving any minute to take over this fiasco and release us from the colonel's custody.

Everyone gets all excited and tries to hold it in but small burst of happiness slips out. Dad takes the paper and writes thank you sheriff and holds it up for the sheriff to see. He shakes his head no and points to Debra and gives her a big thumbs up. Angela grabs her and hugs her and whispers thank you in her ear.

"I'm going to the restroom if you will excuse me for a bit." The sheriff says.

The sheriff removes the paper that he had written on and leaves.

"So how long a ride is it from here to Leavenworth mom?" Harlan asks.

"I'm not sure." Mom says.

Harlan gets a big grin on his face and points at the ceiling to indicate that he is just saying that for the benefit of the colonel.

"It's about three hundred miles, so about four and a half hours." Dad says.

"That's a long trip. I hope we get to stop along the way." Harlan says.

"Really not much to stop at until they get the utilities all up and running again." Henry says.

Debra walks into the room and writes on the paper Homeland Security has just arrived.

"Thanks." Angela says.

"Where is the sheriff?" Debra asks.

"He went to the restroom." Erica replies.

The sheriff walks back in and Debra show's him what she had written. The sheriff nods his head in approval.

"So what else is going on around town?" Henry asks.

"Very little. We are starting to get outsiders coming in and trying to steal stuff like gas, food, water, and even a few horses." The sheriff says.

"Have you checked on our place since we've been in here?" Henry asks.

"Yes I have actually. I checked on them just about every day. The colonel's men seem to be doing a good job of feeding your livestock and no one has broken into your homes. I do think you may have lost some horses Jerry. I swear there seemed to be more of them when I checked the first time but it could be my imagination and I never did count them or anything. I just wanted to make sure everything was secure and that there was feed and water available for them."

The colonel walks into the room followed by the two men from Homeland Security. I have someone here that wants to speak with you people.

"I'm Tom Poulos and this is Jim Harvey we are from the Department of Homeland Security. We would like to talk with you for a bit if we could." Tom says.

"That won't be any problem." The colonel replies.

"You can leave now colonel, we don't need you anymore." Jim says as he ushers the colonel out the door.

"Mr. Poulos, just so you are aware this room is bugged and everything you say can be heard by the colonel." The sheriff says.

"You want to take care of that Jim." Tom says. Jim says "no problem" and walks out of the room.

"First off, on behalf of the President and his staff, I want to apologize for the way that you have been treated. The colonel may have a stellar career on the battlefield but he was most definitely the wrong choice for this position. How and why he was put in this position is a mystery to me but obviously mistakes were made."

Jim walks back into the room and says, "Feel free to say whatever you want now."

"Thanks Jim." Tom says.

"The colonel should be receiving new orders shortly and he will have nothing to do with this operation, nor will he be shipping anyone off to Leavenworth anytime soon."

"Thank you very much." Everyone says.

"Don't thank me thank your sheriff. He is the one that got word to us as to what was going on out here. We have spoken to the sheriff on two or three different occasions and told him if he needed us to let us know.

Anyway, I wish I could say that you could all go back home now, but I can't. We still have a very bad situation here and there are still some very bad people out there that would do you and your families harm. I know that there is no one on this planet that has their children's backs more than their parents and if you say you don't know where they're at right now I'm going to have to live with that.

Let me fill you in on something you don't know and the plan we have to change the game plan so to speak. This facility that you're in is one of the worst kept secrets in the history of histories."

Two men walk in with what looks like electronic sniffing type equipment and start to scan the rooms. One reaches under the sink and pulls out an electronic device that is taped to the underside of the sink. The other guy pulls similar type devices from under the bed, in the mattress and the last one from inside the overhead lighting. They take the stuff and walk out after telling the two agents that all is clear. A third man walks in with a small box with and antenna on it and sets it on the table. He then flips a switch on it and an L.E.D. starts flashing off and on. He says, "You're good to go."

"Thanks." Tom says.

"As you can see there are a lot of people that would like to hear what you guys have to say other than the colonel. According to our information there are more satellites pointed at this building right now than has ever been pointed at the White House. They are watching everything that goes on out here to find out where young Shane and his two friends are hiding.

Now just so you know, this little box that the agent just set on the table is a jamming device. Just in case they missed something. This jams any signals that might be coming out of this room.

So here is what we want to do. We want to move the attention off this place and move it to a more electronically secure place and at the same time try to draw out these people who would do you harm.

Later on this evening, I'll say right around five. A Humvee is going to pull up to the entrance to the facility. Three young people that look like your kids are going to be off loaded and escorted into the facility. As they are brought through the opening between buildings you guys are going to run to them and carry on like your kids have just been returned. You will come back in here. After about thirty minutes the tree <u>kids</u> and six people dressed just like you will be escorted back to the Humvee and will be driven out of here. About thirty minutes after that the seven of you will be transported out of here in the food services truck that is backed up to the far building. During that thirty-minute period you will not say one word to anybody. The success of this operation depends on the bad guys thinking we have moved you. With any luck they will try to intercept the Humvee and we will have them."

"Where are we being moved to?" Henry asks.

"You will be relocated to the Homeland security facility down on Jackson Street. It is very secure and as far as we can tell no one knows it's there. You will stay there until you can be re-united with your kids." Tom says.

"Then what?" Dad asks.

"Well, the President is very unhappy with the way this has gone down. His orders to the colonel were to assess the situation and if it was feasible to obtain this virus and maintain its security then proceed with that. But, if that was not feasible then let it out and get this situation over with.

Obviously Krom doesn't know jack about computers or networks or anything technical. The President said he did not want the recovery process for this country delayed one day because of us trying to develop this into a weapon or keep it to ourselves. Now obviously your son doesn't want his mistake turned into some kind of weapon. I'm going to be honest with you; I think it would be a great tool to have at our disposal. As a matter of fact I told the President those exact words. He told me that it is not worth any delay in getting the country on its feet and besides, if we ask nice this twelve-year-old kid will probably write us a new one. So are we all on the same page with this? Can I count on you? Do you trust me? Tom asks.

CHAPTER TWENTY-EIGHT

THIS IS HOW WE FIX
THE WORLD

Eric unlocks the door and we walk into the bunker. It looks like we just walked into a cross between JPL's command and control center and the deck of the Starship Enterprise. And it's not <u>like</u> a bunker it <u>is</u> a bunker.

"So what do we need to do?" Eric asks Shane.

"Well we need to set up one of your transmitters to transmit on the x band deep space network or the eight-gig high gain frequency." Shane says.

"No problem."

"We will need a way to connect a computer to it and send TCPIP type packets through it."

"Piece of cake." Eric says.

"Then I need to do some coding using the old VxWorks language."

"Do you know that language?" I ask.

"I played around with it a couple of years ago. It was started back in 1985 so there is plenty of info around on it." Shane says.

"But you can't get to that info. No Internet." I said.

"I'll figure it out. In the meantime make sure you don't try the transmitter as a test or anything. We don't want to show or hand. It's only a matter of time before the colonel puts two and two together and figures out where we are. Shane says.

"I'm sure Andy will spill the beans as to what we have in mind." Donna says.

"I know Andy fairly well and he knows I have the ability to do this, so all that colonel has to do is figure out that we are friends and he will be here." Eric says.

"So exactly how does this cocoon work?" Eric asks.

"Well, actually it's really pretty simple."

"Sure it is." I said.

"Really it is. The Monarch virus comes into the computer through the network interface card or NIC as it is commonly referred to. It then installs itself in the computer. After it does some scanning and gathering of information it starts generating what would look like a bunch of garbage and it fills up all the memory in the computer. This is not actually garbage but Monarch is loading the memory chips with the right ones and zeros to create the proper pattern that it needs to destroy it. At the same time it is measuring how big a bang to send out to wipe it all out. Too big a bang and it ends up being shunted by the electronics that supports the memory and to small of a bang and it could leave some chips alive and functioning. When the memory gets full the processor sends out an alert to let the user know he's out of memory. This alert triggers Monarch and Monarch generates what is basically a system wide EMF pulse that exceeds the limits of the reverse bias that a chip can handle. This destroys the chip or all the chips leaving the computer useless."

"See I told you it was simple." I say while laughing.

"The Monarch is an intelligent virus. One of the reason it scans everything is that it is determining what kind of device it's living on. If it determines it is a switch or router it doesn't destroy it but sets up shop and then replicates itself and attaches itself to anything that passes through it. Of course this infects every computer, workstation, embedded processor, or whatever, that touches that switch or router and then it gets passed on to other routers and switches and so on and so on.

The Monarch has some really powerful and somewhat nasty defense mechanisms built into it. Basically you can't destroy it without destroying the device. Some of these devices are very inaccessible and you can't just turn them off or replace them.

So when the cocoon is released, it encases Monarch on any switch or router it touches, fooling it into thinking nothing is passing through it. That stops the spread of Monarch through them. It then replicates itself and attaches itself to the proper packets as they go through the switch or router. When that packet gets to its destination cocoon installs itself on the computer and basically builds a digital cocoon around the Monarch virus and makes it think that there is always free memory. The computer never sends out an alert that it's out of memory and Monarch never triggers the destruct phase. Monarch will still be on the computer but this will protect any computer from being destroyed until Monarch can be totally eradicated, which will probably take years. One small problem is that the Monarch residing in the switch or router will eventually figure out that it is being by passed and it will figure a way around the cocoon. Hopefully by the time that happens all the computers that are up and running will be protected by the cocoon." Shane replies.

"Will the cocoon that is on the computer ever figure out that it's being tricked and destroy its host?" Eric asks.

"No it shouldn't. It knows it's on a computer and it shouldn't be doing any testing. It's just waiting for and out of memory alert."

"So what if the user actually runs out of memory?" Molly asks.

"That wouldn't be good." Shane says.

"It would trigger Monarch." I said.

"Yep."

"I would suggest that all the software companies send out a patch that disables that alert then." Eric says.

"There was a part of the virus that I never finished so I don't know if it works and let's hope it doesn't."

"What was it?" I ask.

"If monarch detects that the alert has been disabled, it will set itself off. I don't think that will function. I never got to test it."

"Oh my God. Why? You have to share with us your thought process that went into developing this. How does one set down at a computer and say, ok I'm bored so I want to create something that will destroy things." I said.

"That's really not what happened." Shane says.

"I want to be a network security specialist when I grow up. To really get a good job in network security you have to be good at securing a network. Networks are most vulnerable to hackers. People who deliberately break into a network to steal something whether it be a bank account passwords, top secret information, or even time."

"Time?" I ask.

"Yes time. There are people out there that are selling processing power to companies and they hack into some big computer like at a university, or whoever they can steal it from.

My point is that there are people trying to break in to other people's computers. So a network security guy's job is to prevent them from getting in. To do this he needs to know how to hack in himself to be able to figure out a way to stop them. So I have to think like a hacker. A hacker wants to get in, get what he wants, and destroy any evidence that he was ever there. So I have to design viruses and exploits that do all sort of devious things to be able to know what to look for and how to stop it."

"That's really boring. I like my portrayal of you better. You know bored and maniacal." I said.

"Sorry to disappoint you." Shane says.

"Can we get on with saving the world, people? I'm sure we will read all about Shane's story when the newspapers can print again." Donna says.

"Sure. I need to set up a computer and start figuring out the code I need to push to the rover." Shane says.

"There are two workstations here and my personal laptop none of which has connected to your Internet of doom so they should be ok." Eric says.

"Great, we may have to sacrifice one of them to test this out." Shane says.

"Really? In that case I will go into the house and get my mother's laptop." Eric says.

"That's mean." Molly says.

"She doesn't have Terabytes of data stored on hers." Eric says.

"If this doesn't work and it destroys her laptop we have a lot bigger problem on our hands than destroying your mother's laptop." Shane says.

"Do you have Python running on any of them?" Shane asks.

"It's running on all of them." Eric says.

"I should have known that." Shane says while chuckling.

"Anyway I'll use this workstation until we are ready to test it. The tough part is trying to retrieve the code off of Abby's iPod. If it copied it over as binary file then we are in good shape, if it actually copied it as an audio file then we may be screwed."

"Just don't blow up my iPod please. It was a gift from mom and dad and I don't want you working your magic on it and destroying it." I said.

"Man, don't you ever let up?" Shane asks.

I laugh and say, "After this is all over with, you are going to replace my computer at home, and my TV."

"I have a feeling if people ever find out it was me they will all want me to replace all of their computers."

"Ok I have the transmitter tuned and ready to go all you need to do is plug it into the USB port on the computer. The antenna is phased perfectly and the pre amps are all warmed up and ready to go. All we have to do is bring the power up." Eric says.

"Ok now get another transmitter set up to use when we try and reach the International Space Station." Shane says.

"Roger that. I'm thinking that they are not going to be a lot of people trying to contact them right now so we might have a chance of getting through." Eric says.

"Even if we don't actually make contact with them, there should be people around the world listening for any kind of communication from the space station and they will hear our broadcast to them. Then they will know to try and receive the broadcast from the rover. We really only need two or three countries to hear us." Shane says.

"I hope we make contact because if we do, and they repeat what we say to them, then it will reach a lot more stations around the world." Eric says.

"Ok Abby let me see your iPod." Shane says.

"It will still have the music on it when you're done right?" I say as I slowly take the iPod off of my wrist.

"I promise it will be fine." Shane says.

Shane takes the iPod and plugs the computer cable into it. He hits the enter button and files start to scroll down the screen. When they stop scrolling he unplugs the iPod and hands it back to Abby.

"See, it's fine." Shane says.

"I never doubted you for a minute." I said.

Eric looks at the screen and scrolls up and down.

"There is the music and wow, there's the cocoon!"

"Is it useable though?" Eric asks.

"It looks just like it did when I saved it on the DVD so it may be ok. Let's see if I can open it. Keep your fingers crossed." Shane says.

Shane sets down in front of the computer and opens up the Python Software and then tries to import the file. The computer sets there for what seems like an eternity and then starts displaying the contents of the file.

"Oh my God it's still useable! I wonder if Apple knows you can do that." Shane says.

"You mean its ok." Donna says.

"Yes indeed it's ok." Shane says.

A cheer goes up and there are high fives going around the room. Shane gets up and starts hugging me. We realize what we are doing and stop with a look of embarrassment. Then I say, "what the heck" and grab Shane and we hug and dance around the room. Molly says "what the heck" and grabs Eric and they start hugging and dancing around the room.

CHAPTER TWENTY-NINE

THE FIX IS IN

"Well since your mother's laptop survived the test I guess there is nothing left to do but try it." Shane says.

"The space station should be visible fairly soon." Eric says.

"How are we going to know if it works?" I ask.

"That's a good question." Shane replies.

"I have an ideal that could not only verify that it was received by the rover but also help in the retransmitting." Eric says.

"Let's hear what you got."

"I have a friend that lives out in Vegas. His name is Joel Flowers. He is a big time ham radio guy and has a crazy set up out there. It's all solar powered and it's located on top of a mountain out there call Black Mountain. He has relays that cover northern Arizona, Southern Utah, Southern Nevada, and all of Southern California. He also manages the emergence broadcast system out there in Vegas. We communicate almost daily. I can send him an encrypted message telling him what we are doing."

"Isn't sending encrypted message over Ham Radio illegal?" Shane asks.

"We are getting ready to hack into a two and a half billion dollar piece of government property setting on mars and you are worried about me sending an encrypted message using ham radio." Eric says.

"Guess you're right, carry on." Shane says.

"Anyway, we can send it right after we start the rover uplink, in case big brother is listening. He can then monitor the rover transmissions and see if he can capture the re-transmission. If he can, he can notify us that it was a success, and then start re-broadcasting the rover broadcast to all those places in the western U.S."

"I would suggest that we get ready to get you guys out of here as soon as we send the transmission. I'm sure they will be here shortly thereafter." Donna says. "Unless of course you are ready to give yourself up. If this works, I'm sure they will have no reason to keep you or your parents anymore. But that's up to you."

"Actually I'm ready to be back with my mom and dad so I think if it works then we can just wait for them to get here." Shane says.

"Really?" I said.

"Yes, I want to go home." Shane says.

"Me too." Molly says.

"But we still need to be ready to get out of here just in case it doesn't work. I wouldn't want to go back out to the ranch and not be able to continue trying to make it work." Shane says.

"It will work." I said.

"I think we should keep our options open." Donna says.

"What do you mean?" I ask.

"I think we should bail out of here just as soon as we send the signal. That way we have the opportunity to try something else, because it seems to me that even if everything works correctly there could be other issues that we haven't thought of.

If we just sit here and let them pick you up we have lost any ability to try again." Donna says.

"Wow the sheriff's wife is starting to sound like a criminal, just like the rest of us." I said.

"But she does make sense, so let's plan on getting out of here. But first let's find out if it's going to work." Shane says.

"I've written out a script for you to read Eric. You don't have to say exactly what it says word for word, but it just says what we need to get across so say it however you want to." Shane says.

"Cool, so how do you want to time this?" Eric says.

"Go ahead and bring up the transmitters. I will wait until you have made contact and then I will hit the transmit key on both transmitters and the enter key on the computer. If you haven't made contact after five minutes then just make a general broadcast to whoever is out there and I'll go ahead and send it to the rover and the space station anyway. Maybe someone will get it and switch over and record the data from one of them, nothing else your friend in Vegas will get it and rebroadcast it."

"The space station will be visible in thirty-nine seconds. It is going to be about 30 degrees off the horizon so we want have very long to communicate with them. So let's do this thang!" Eric says.

Eric sets down in front of the radio and Shane walks over to the other radios and puts his hand on the transmit buttons. Then Eric begins.

"November Alpha One Sierra Sierra this is AE7BX calling, you guys awake up there?"

There is a long pause and no reply.

"November Alpha One Sierra Sierra this is AE7BX calling, this is AE7BX calling the International Space Station can you guys hear me up there?"

Another long pause and then "This is Colonel Zayo welcome aboard the International Space Station. Didn't think we would be hearing from anybody down there for a while."

"Roger that Colonel it is awesome to make contact with you but we only have a couple minutes here so I need for you to give me a listen."

"OK AE7BX what's up?"

"Colonel you should be receiving an APRS format packet transmission at the same time I'm talking here. We are sending you an antivirus program that will stop the Monarch virus from spreading any further and protect any new systems. We are simultaneously pushing this same data to and trough the Mars Rover Curiosity. Anyone hearing this broadcast should tune to the download link frequency of 900 megahertz and capture the data and resend it, make CD copies of it, distribute it any way they can. I repeat anyone hearing this broadcast should capture the data being broadcast from the Mars Rover at 900 megahertz or the packet retransmission from the space station at 145.800 megahertz. Capture it and redistribute it anyway possible over."

There is a long pause.

"AE7BX this is the space station have we just been hi jacked over?"

"I'm sorry colonel but this is the only way we can get this sent out over."

"So this is real. This will fix the virus over?"

"Yes sir it is. Guaranteed over."

"Roger that AE7BX we will re-broadcast until they tell us to stop, November Alpha One Sierra Sierra 73."

"Thanks colonel AE7BX 73."

We all break into shouting and high fives are flying around the room.

"We did it." Eric shouts.

"We sure did!" I reply with a shout.

"Let's not get too excited. It will take fourteen minutes for the signal to get to the rover and fourteen more for it to get back to us. We won't know if we succeeded for twenty-eight more minutes." Shane says.

"When Joel receives the signal out there in Vegas he is supposed to send me a set of tones and we will hear them on my portable that is attached to my belt so let's get out of here while we can." Eric says.

As they start to walk out a voice comes over the radio. AE7BX KF7EDU.

"Who the heck is that?" I ask.

Eric walks over to the radio and picks up the mike.

"KF7EDU this is AE7BX."

"AE7BX please be advised that I have received the packet broadcast from the Space Station and will make copies to distribute as soon as I can get a computer with a burner up and running. Also be advised that Colonel Krom and a convoy of small trucks left here and is headed to your location. You should have about forty-five minutes before they arrive. KF7EDU AE7BX 73."

"Thanks KF7EDU AE7BX 73."

"Let's get out of here!" Donna says.

"Wait, who was that?" I said.

"KF7EDU is a preacher in Perry." Eric says.

"Pastor Gleason?" I ask.

"That would be correct."

"Awesome." I said.

"We have to go." Donna says.

Eric kills all the power to the bunker and we all head for the sheriff's car. It's going to be a little snug but we can all fit.

"I'm just going to stay here. I live here and I want to make sure they don't trash the place looking for clues to where we went." Eric says.

"It's your call." Donna says.

We all hug Eric and thank him.

"I'm sorry I drug you into this." Shane says to Eric.

"Don't be sorry. I'm glad you did. You know me; anytime I can put one over on the PoPo I'm happy." Eric says.

"Thanks man." Shane says and hugs Eric one more time.

"Here take this." Eric hands Shane the portable radio that was hanging on his belt.

"Just listen for the tones. If the colonel doesn't haul me away I'll call you on it and let you know when he leaves here."

We get in the car and pull out of the driveway.

"We are going to take the back roads. I'm sure that the colonel was able to hear the preachers broadcast so they are going to be watching for us on the main road, but I don't think he has enough men to watch all the roads. Or, we can go into the city. I know the sheriff there and we could hang out there until we receive the conformation tones." Donna says.

"No, let's go home." I said.

"I agree." Shane and Molly reply.

"Ok then everybody hang on." Donna says.

Donna seemed to know how to drive on the back roads very well and was making real good time.

"How much longer before we should hear something?" I ask.

"Three minutes left then the signal will have had time to get there and back. That can be off by a few minutes either way. Then we don't know how long it will take for the guy in Vegas to send out the tones." Shane says.

"Why is he sending out tones, why doesn't he just say hey I received the program?" Molly asked.

"He is just sending out the tones because nobody will know what it means or who sent it. It will be short so that it can't be traced. That way his cover is not blown and he can crank out copies of the antivirus without them shutting him down." I said.

"Wow Abby, you're getting really good at this stuff." Shane says.

"I pay attention." I said.

"So what are we going to do when we get back?" Molly asks.

"Well if the transmission was a successful, then I guess we go out to the ranch and see the Colonel. If it wasn't we continue to hide out and come up with some way to get the message out." I said.

"Well we just past twenty-eight minutes so the signal should have made it there and back. JPL has also had time to send the rover a stop command to stop it from transmitting. Of course even if it stops transmitting now we should still receive packets for fourteen more minutes." Shane says.

Fifteen more minutes passed by and you could feel the excitement slowly draining away. It was very quiet in the car and no one wanted to be the first to say I guess we failed. Then Donna spoke up and said, "We are only twenty minutes from the house so everyone be ready, because when we get a little closer I want everyone to get down so no one can see you. I will pull into the garage and close the door then everyone can get out."

As Donna was explaining what to do the little radio came to life. Two very weird and very loud tones came blasting out of the speaker.

"Oh my God it worked!" I screamed.

We all started screaming and bouncing up and down. Donna was so excited that she had to pull the car over on the side of the road.

"Wow, I can't believe that we were able to use the International Space Station and the Curiosity Rover on Mars to do this." Shane said.

"It's insane. Let's just hope that a lot of people were listening and were able to receive the antivirus." I said.

Donna pulls back onto the road and starts driving.

"Even though you have been successful I think you should still give it a little time before we go to the Colonel. So let's go to the house as planned. So everybody get down because we are here."

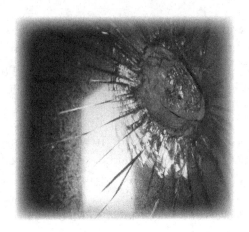

CHAPTER THIRTY

SHATTERED GLASS
IS IN THIS YEAR

Everyone got down as low as possible as we got to the sheriff's house. She pulled up in front of the garage and hit the button on the garage door opener. Nothing happened.

"I forgot there is no power to the garage door without the generator running." Donna says.

A car pulls in behind them.

"Oh crap. Who's that? Let me get out and draw their attention away from the car. I will go into the house just like I was getting home normally. I'll see who it is and what they want. Everyone stay down." Donna says.

Donna gets out of the car and walks back to their car. We hear what sounds like two men get out of the car behind us and then we hear Donna say, "So what brings Homeland Security out tonight?"

"We heard you were seen up near Oklahoma City today. You sure get around don't you," one of the men says.

"Yes I was up that way taking care of some business."

We hear the front door open.

"So why don't you gentlemen come on in the house if you want to talk. It's too cold out here and I have to start up the generator so I can pull my car into the garage." Donna says.

"That would be fine." One of them says.

"I'm Tom by the way and this is Jim." Donna then escorts them into the house.

"Make yourself at home."

She walks over to a control panel on the wall by the utility room and pushes a button to start the generator.

"I need to pull the car into the garage so I can shut that generator down." Donna says.

She then walks out and gets in the car.

"Ok guys I'm going to pull into the garage and shut the door. I will keep them in the den and ya'll try to sneak in through the utility room. I'll see what they want and try to get rid of them."

Donna pulls the car into the garage and gets out and shuts the garage door.

"Ok guys let's try to get to the utility room. If we get to the utility room then we can go down into the cellar and stay there until they leave." I said.

"Why don't we just walk in and say WERE HERE and see what they do." Shane says.

"Because they probably don't know that the antivirus is now being distributed around the world. It's going to take a little while before the authorities know what has happened. In the mean time they are going to lock us up somewhere and I don't want to be lock up again." I said.

"She says as we try to make our way to locking ourselves in a root cellar." Molly says.

"I agree with her. We need to keep cool and see what happens for the next twenty-four hours." Shane says.

I slowly open the door that leads from the garage to the utility room. We very quietly sneak into the utility room and

I grab the clothes hamper. As I push it over a light comes on down in the basement and the steps leading down are exposed.

"Let's go." I whisper and start down the steps.

Molly follows, and then Shane. Shane reaches up and pulls the clothes hamper back in place.

"I still think we need to be as quiet as possible so no one hears us down here." Molly says.

"Very true." I said.

"Turn up the speaker so we can listen in on what's going on up stairs." I said.

Molly reaches over and turns up the volume until they can hear Donna's voice.

"I went up to visit a friend and make sure him and his family were doing ok." Donna says.

"And that was Eric Hill right?" One of the men asks.

"That is right." Donna says.

"Why didn't you just call him on the radio? He is a Ham Radio operator isn't he?"

"I believe he is, but I don't have a Ham Radio and he probably doesn't have a police band radio." Donna says.

"So why don't you just cut to the chase, what are you here for?" Donna asks.

"We are here to find Shane Bevil and the two girls and I'm pretty sure you know where they are. Mrs. Hardery you do understand that you are hindering federal agents from doing their job and I could arrest you, just like the colonel did your husband, right here on the spot." Tom says.

"I haven't lied to you and have invited you into my home to try and help you so I don't see that as hindering you." Donna says.

"So you are going to sit right there and tell me you don't know where these kids are."

"Gentlemen I think it's time you left. You have worn out you welcome." Donna says.

Donna stands up and walks to the front door. The two men get up and start to walk out.

"You do know we are the good guys right?" Jim asks Donna.

"I know that everyone thinks they are doing the right thing for their country and that makes them think they are the good guys."

"Well one of those good guys is your husband and we had a nice talk to him today. He said to tell you that the colonel is now out of the picture and that you could trust us." Tom says.

"Sure he did." Donna says.

"He said you would say that to. He also said you need to come out and talk to him as soon as possible. I think he is going to like what you did to his car. I hear shattered glass is in this year." Tom says.

The two men walk out to their car and leave. As they drive off Donna turns toward the utility room and says "you guys can come up now."

I open the trap door and we go up and into the kitchen.

"I'm sorry Donna we didn't mean for you to get into all this trouble." I said.

"Don't worry about it. I think time will prove that we did what was right. So what do you guys want to do? I think we have done all we can do at this point. Your plan either worked or it didn't, but I don't think we could pull off trying something else. Not when they are killing people in my front yard." Donna says.

"I think we need to go out to the ranch." Shane says.

"I need to see mom and dad and make sure they are all right." I said.

"Yea me too." Molly says.

"Yea but how do we get there?" I ask.

"What do you mean?" Donna asks.

"Obviously we can't just roll up out there in your car with you driving. That would be very incriminating for you. That would kind of tell them that you really did know where we were all this time." I said.

"Believe me, if they knew we were at Eric Hill's house in Oklahoma City then they know you are here." Donna says.

"Then why didn't they just take us when they were here?" I said.

"I don't know. It's weird. Anyway don't worry about me. I'll just say I picked you up on the way out there."

"Well, do we all agree, it's time to give it up.

Shane?

"Yes."

Molly?

"Yes."

Donna? "Yes."

"I guess I make it unanimous. Besides if that dude was telling us the truth then the colonel is no longer running things so it might be totally different." I said.

"True." Donna says.

"Do you guys want one last meal before we go?" Donna asks.

"No way." Molly says.

"I couldn't eat even if you forced me to." Shane says.

"No." I said.

"Then let's head out." Donna says.

I grab Donna and hug her. Molly and Shane quickly join me.

"Ok I think until we get out of the area we should stay down and out of site in the car. That way it will give credence to Donna's story that she picked us up on the way out there to see the sheriff." I said.

"I agree." Donna says.

"But wait. Where did you pick us up at?" Molly asks.

"On the square, that way you don't have to stay hidden very long." Donna says.

Once again they head for the garage and get down in the floorboard as Donna pulls the car out. She drives off and heads for the square. She makes a quick drive by of the square and then tells everyone it's time to get up. They head for the ranch. About a mile from the ranch Donna says, "Ok this is it. If you want to back out, now is the time, we get any closer we can't turn back".

No one says anything.

"Guys say something." Donna says.

"Keep on going." I said.

"Let's do this thang!" Molly says.

As Donna pulls up to the ranch they notice that there doesn't appear to be anyone there.

"That's weird." I said.

"Look, the front security gate is standing wide open."

Donna stops the car and they get out and walk in. Everything is gone. All that is left is the buildings.

"What the heck?" Shane says?

"Where did everybody go?" I ask.

We walk through each building and find nothing. As we are looking we here a commotion outside. We walk to the nearest window and see two black sedans parked out front and what looks like six guys getting out.

"Oh crap." Donna says.

"I don't think those guys are here to help us. We need to get out of here." I say.

"How, they are parked all around our car?" Shane says.

"Let's head toward the back building."

As we start moving back we hear what sounds like a helicopter come in overhead.

"Great now were screwed." Donna says.

A voice comes over a loud speaker that appears to be coming from the helicopter. The voice commands them to put down their weapons. A quick peak out a window reveals that the colonel has pulled up with a number of his men. The next thing we hear is gunshots. A lot of gunshots. Coming from both the colonel's men and the helicopter.

"Run to the back!" Donna yells.

We all start running and make it to the back door. As luck would have it it's locked.

"Great." Donna says.

She starts trying to kick it open.

"Listen. The shooting has stopped." I said.

"Let's hope we won." Molly says.

Donna stops trying to kick open the door and we all become very quiet and try to hear what is going on. We hear loud footsteps coming our way and with an explosive type force the door leading into the room fly's open. Two soldiers rush in pointing their weapons at the four of us who are cowering on the floor in front of the locked back door. Molly starts screaming, "Don't shoot."

The colonel walks in and tells the soldiers to stand down.

"Well, well the colonel says. Didn't expect to see you out here today. Glad you could drop by. You're all under arrest."

A voice comes booming in from behind the colonel and it says, "No there not". Tom from Homeland Security steps in and says. "Colonel you need to go out and take care of the mess outside. These four people are no longer any of your concern."

The colonel flares up and says, "I don't think so."

"Colonel. Do you really want to speak to a superior officer that way?" Tom asks.

"Superior officer." The colonel says. "Don't make me laugh."

"Oh maybe I need to introduce myself. I'm Major General Tom Poulos United States Marine Corp. I have been assigned to the Pentagon as a liaison between Homeland Security and the Marine Corp. I'm currently acting as a division chief for Homeland Security at the request of the White House. Now that we have been properly introduced I would suggest you get your butt in gear and get outside with your men."

The colonel snaps a short salute and says, "Yes sir." He then walks out and tells his men to follow him.

CHAPTER THIRTY-ONE

LET'S GO HOME

"I have a feeling the colonel has a lot of explaining to do. If I were a betting man I would bet that the next time you see him you will address him as Sergeant Krom."

Tom reaches down and offers his hand to me to help me get up.

"Now Donna don't you think it would have been a lot easier if you would have just handed them over to me when I asked you to."

"Actually I found them at the park and convinced them to come out here." Donna says.

"Oh really. So you are actually the hero in all of this, not the villain?" Tom says.

"I didn't say that."

"I won't even get into the fact, that just as soon as you passed the park, three extra heads popped up in your car and you hadn't even stopped."

"No comment." Donna says.

"Yea I think it's best that you don't comment. Now I take it that you're Shane?"

He holds out his hand to shake Shane's hand.

"Yes sir." Shane says.

"And based on the resemblance to your mother I'm going to say your Abby."

"Yes sir." I say as I stick out my hand to take his.

"So that leaves Molly."

Tom says and reaches over to shake Molly's hand.

"Yes sir I'm Molly."

"I'm not going to waste any more time. I know that you are ready to see your parents so we are going to take you to them.

Now we still have a security issue. Obviously some people, like the ones laying all over the ground out there, haven't got the memo yet telling them you guys pulled off, one of the slickest moves I've ever heard of, and actually high jacked the Mars Rover and broadcast your files all over the world and that they don't need to kidnap you anymore.

So, until they do get the message, we are going to have to act like they are still out there looking for you. So I have to figure a way to get you to your parents without others knowing where you are hiding.

If you will give me a few minutes I will figure it out. Oh yea did I tell you guys that I'm really thankful that the four of you are on our side." Tom says and starts laughing as he walks away.

He tells one of the soldiers, "Sergeant make sure everybody stays back here. They may be super ninjas when it comes to avoiding us but there still twelve year old kids and they don't need to see that mess up front."

"Yes sir." The soldier says.

"Well it sounds like this may be over. Getting to go back home will be awesome. Of course it won't be the same without Zoe and Murdock. I really love those horses." I said.

"You never know, they may be around here somewhere. I'm sure the sheriff will find them once he gets back into doing his job." Donna says.

"You know they still hang horse thieves in these here parts." Molly says.

"One thing for sure our lives will never be the same." I said.

"Mine sure won't. I have to live the rest of my life thinking about all those people that have suffered or died as a result of what I did." Shane says.

"Look, you didn't do it on purpose and a lot of the tragedy that has taken place is because of people doing stupid things not because you did what you did." Donna says.

"She's right." I said.

"People going ballistic and burning buildings and hurting each other is because they are nuts not because their computers don't work." Molly says.

"I appreciated you guys saying that, and I understand what you are saying, but the bottom line is I caused all of this and I will go down in the history books as the one that caused all this."

Tom walks back into the room and says, "Ok guys I commandeered the colonels Humvee and we are going to take you to your parents. The vehicle will pull around to this door and you get in as quick as possible. I'm sure by now the bad guys know your here and will watch where we are taking you so we have three vehicles. Two decoys and one you will actually be in. I hope that this will confuse them and slow them down enough that it will give us enough time to get the word out that the antivirus is available. The President is going on the air in about an hour and a half to announce to the world via emergency broadcast and analog satellite transmissions that the antivirus is available to anyone that wants it and his communications chief will follow right behind him and tell people how and where to get it."

"It looks like you guys pulled it off." Tom says. "It will soon be over."

Shane's eyes start to tear up and he just shakes his head.

"Aren't you going to arrest me or press charges against me?" Shane asks.

"No. You didn't do this on purpose. It was an accident. Besides you're only twelve years old. Can you imagine the bad press that the President would get if he tried to prosecute a twelve-year-old boy that accidentally killed the Internet?

If anything he will spin it that this has been an eye-opening event. That our country and others countries have a lot of work to do to get us away from depending so much on a system that can so drastically fail. A system so fragile that a twelve-year-old boy could use it to bring the world to its knees. Accidentally of course. Ok your ride is here." Tom says.

A soldier opens the door and motions for us to come on.

"Mrs. Hardery these three youngsters have to go with me in the Humvee, however, you are free to go. I can't force you to go with us but I think you should." Tom says.

"Oh I'm going with you." Donna says.

"If you would like I can have one of my men bring the sheriff's car with us so you and the sheriff will have transportation when you are ready to go home." Tom says.

"That would be great, but would it be ok if I drove it and just followed you." Donna says.

"Works for me. Alright then let's load up." Tom says.

We all start climbing into the awaiting Humvee hopefully to never return to such a beautiful ranch under such ugly conditions.

Molly makes her way into the Humvee and sits next to Shane. I motion for Molly to move so that I can sit next to Shane. As the Humvee makes its way to our parents, I decide it's time to discuss the pictures of me that we had found on his laptop.

"So Shane, I'm sorry that I put your laptop in the water trough and that it was destroyed by Krom's men." I said.

"No problem. It wasn't your fault they destroyed it." Shane says.

"I know. But, speaking of your laptop, you know that Molly went through it pretty thoroughly trying to find a clue as to where you were or what had happened to you, Right?" I said.

"Yea, so?"

"You seem to have a lot of pictures on it. As a matter of fact that was about all that was on it, you know, except for the music files." I said.

"Oh crap!" Shane says as he turns a very bright shade of red.

"Busted!" Molly says.

"So, I have a lot of pictures, it's no big deal." Shane says.

"I'm not talking about the number of pictures you have. Or had. I'm talking about the ones of me. Specifically the ones of me that someone had Photoshopped." I said.

"Yea the ones that said you lovvvved her." Molly says.

"Will you be quiet?" I tell Molly.

Shane turns and looks out the window ignoring both Molly and I.

Tom is setting in the front and he turns around to talk to us.

"You need to understand that this is far from over. Even after the President makes his speech there will still be people out there that have suffered because of this and they may lash out in anger at the three of you. Especially at Shane."

"But really, how many people actually know who it was that caused this and that Molly and I were involved in it at all?" I said.

"Well the President plans on focusing on the re-building process and what has to happen and how the government will be helping people get through this.

He is also going to make sure that everyone knows that the foreign agents that illegally entered the county were arrested and that he will be pursuing legal action against them with the full might of the U.S. government. Even though the arrest weren't connected to the actual cause of the disaster it will give people someone or something to direct their anger at. This should turn most people's attention away from the witch-hunt of looking for the bad guys and hopefully it will be long enough to give people time to cool down some.

It will be awhile before the news establishment gets back up and running so that will buy you some time also.

All the soldiers involved at the camp are under orders not to say a word about any of this. They will face prison time if they do. The colonel is too good a soldier to say anything. By that I mean he will stick to the code when it comes to something like this. He is definitely not a good soldier.

We probably don't have to worry about the foreign governments saying anything. Odds are they are going to keep quiet to protect their own since they would have to admit that they were actually here.

You and your families are going to have to come up with answers to those people you are involved with on a day to day bases. Specifically other family members like relatives.

The bottom line is that it will eventually get out that Shane, caused this. Hopefully it will take some time for that to happen and by then I think most people will have turned their anger toward the government for letting us get in this situation and not having a plan. However, I do think that Shane and his family will need to disappear for a while. Not forever but long enough for people to get back into living again."

The Humvee pulls up to the Homeland security facility. A set of overhead doors open and the driver pulls the Humvee inside.

"Ok guys let's get out and see if there is anyone here that's anxious to see you." Tom says.

As we start getting out I hear someone start screaming and I look up to see my mom leading the charge as our parents realize we are there. I don't think I have ever been hugged as hard by my mom and dad nor have I cried as hard as I did then.

After about fifteen minutes Tom walks over to an open door and starts waving his hand.

"If I can get everyone to follow me, we need to move into the lunch room area. We have a monitor set up and we will be able to watch the Presidents speech. So follow me."

Everyone starts to move toward the open door in a shuffling kind of way because no one was willing to let go or stop hugging.

The room was kind of small and it had six tables and four vending machines crammed into it. At one end of the room and in front of the vending machines they had set a large flat screen T.V. on a table. There was an image of the Presidential seal on the screen and you could hear random voices coming from the speakers. Tom walks over and stands in front of the T.V.

"If everyone would take a seat the President's speech should start very shortly. Remember that due to the lack of working equipment around the country this will be a very limited broadcast mostly only received by government facilities at this time but as they get equipment up and working around the country it will be re-broadcasted to them."

On the screen we see the President walk up to the podium and start to speak.

"I'm here today to share with you information that I know you all have been waiting to hear. Mainly that an antivirus is now available to everyone that, if done properly, will kill the virus that has destroyed millions of computers around the world.

Over the past few days this country as well as other countries around the world has been locked in an epic battle. Not against some warring faction trying to do us harm but against the failure of our own technology and the lack of importance and respect that this administration and previous administrations have given that technology. A technology that we as a people have gradually let take control of our lives.

First off I want to make sure everyone knows that the failure of the network infrastructure was not caused by some sort of Cyber Terrorism as we first thought. Although the failure brought a lot of terrorist types illegally into our country to try and capitalize on it, it was not caused by terrorist. It was caused by a virus that was sent by a twelve-year-old boy to another twelve-year-old boy to try and get even for a wrong that had been done against him. It never was meant to harm anyone. It was never meant to cause the destruction that it has caused. It was never meant for it to spread the way that it did. So the bottom line is that it was an accident.

I call on all of the brilliant engineering minds out there to come together and determine just how this was able to happen, and make sure it can never happens again.

What I want everyone else to focus on now is getting our country back up and running. People do not need to go off on some witch-hunt to try and punish the one that caused this. The foreign agents that illegally entered this country were arrested and will be prosecuted to the full extent of the law.

Technology, or the use of that technology, failed us but there is one thing that I feel is even more important that we try to understand and deal with. As human beings we need to understand and fix whatever it is that brought this great <u>civilized</u> nation to the point that we are at today.

Thousands of people have died needlessly. There have been billions of dollars in property damage. Family businesses burnt to the ground. <u>Trains,</u> the one mode of transportation that we would have been able to get back up and running the quickest, were set on fire and burned. Destroyed.

This wasn't caused by a twelve year old kid releasing a virus on the Internet. This was caused by some sort of condition or anger that lies within people that emerges when they get scared or maybe it's when things don't go the way <u>they</u> think they should be going. I don't understand this but we as a nation need to understand it and deal with it.

I also want everyone to understand that if you are guilty of causing someone harm or destroying property during this time you will be prosecuted and there will be no temporary insanity pleas or blaming it on the virus. You will pay for your actions.

As your President I vow that I will do what's necessary to get this country back up and running again. I also vow that this country will no longer be at the mercy of something as fragile and as un-forgiving as the Internet and our National Network Infrastructure.

We have a long road ahead of us. In the coming days I will be putting in place some temporary laws and regulations that will help us to get back into full operation. Some of you are not going to like this, but I assure you it is best for our country.

Before I end this broadcast I would like to acknowledge some of the people who were responsible for getting the antivirus out to the public to help bring and end to this disaster.

I can't condone the method that they used to accomplish this because it involved hijacking billions of dollars worth of equipment owned by the Federal Government, and I don't particularly agree with the final outcome, but I have to stand in awe of what they pulled off and I have to admire them for doing what they thought was right.

Before they were taken hostage by the Chinese and were able to orchestrate their escape by outwitting the Chinese agents, they successfully obtained the only existing copy of the antivirus and kept it out of the hands of the bad guys.

Then, with the help of a very courageous woman, these two young ladies, who are only twelve years old, out maneuvered the military and several other U.S. Government agents, and then made a very dangerous cross country trip to a location that they could use to transmit the antivirus. I should also mention that the young boy that originally released this virus is the one that figured out how to fix it and how to broadcast it to the world and yes he was also a part of cross country road trip.

I would love to tell you their names but, due to their age and me not having their parents' permission, I can't. I'm sure that their whole story will come out as time goes on. Someone is sure to write a book about it.

I am now going to turn this over to my communications chief who will give you details on how to obtain and use the antivirus.

I ask each and every one of you to pray for our country. Thank you.

After the speech ended everyone started hugging again and everyone started thanking Donna and the sheriff for all they had done. Donna managed to get free from the pile of people around her and came over to talk to me.

"I have some great news for you Abby."

"Really, what's that?"

"On my way over here deputy Murphy called on the radio and told me that they had found your horses. He said they found them tied up behind the Library and that they were taking them back home for you."

"That's fantastic. I thought they were probably gone forever."

Tom walks over to the center of the room.

"If I can have everyone's attention for a moment. My security people have informed me that since the word is now out, and that there is now no value in any information that you might have, that with the exception of Shane and his family, we will be allowing everyone else to leave."

A loud roar of approval breaks out around the room.

"We feel that the only thing anyone would be interested in at this time is the laptop and we have made sure that everyone knows that we have it not you guys.

If any of you would feel better staying with us a while that is certainly understandable and we will make arrangements.

Also, to be on the safe side, we will assign a security detail to keep an eye on you and your homes for the next week or two, but you are free to return home."

"Why can't Shane go home?" I asked.

"We feel that it is best that Shane and his family disappear for awhile. We will temporally relocate them until we feel it is safe for them to return. I'm sorry, I know that is one of the main things you guys were trying to prevent, but I promise you that this will only be for a short period of time.

One more thing. It is very important that you remain quiet about this at this time. Be careful who you talk to. Be very careful what you say and who you say it to.

With that being said I would ask you to get into the Humvee of your choice so that you can be taken home or wherever you would like to go."

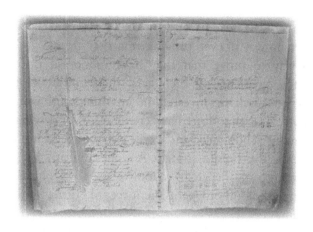

CHAPTER THIRTY-TWO

SO LET IT BE WRITTEN

Well the president was right. Someone had to write a book about all this and I figured I was in the best position to do so.

It's been a little over a two months since the Monarch reign of terror came to an end. The power and water are back on in most places but the schools, banks and financial institutions are all still shut down.

It appears that Monarch was even nastier than anyone thought. Seems the EMP that was supposed to take out the memory and the processors also bled over into the hard drives and corrupted most of them as well. Most people thought that once they replaced the computer all they would have to do was copy their data off the old drive and be back in business. Not so.

Across the country things are still really bad. Living on this farm I'm sheltered from most of the stuff that is going on out there in the real world. We still have food and things to get by on. People out there on the other hand have no money and even worse they have no <u>data</u> and by that I mean in a lot of cases they have no way of even proving who they are.

No way to prove that they have money in the bank, or have made payments on their cars, their houses, or that they ever owned stock or invested in anything. I'm worried that even those of us that don't have credit cards, or driving records, you know us school aged kids, will also suffer greatly from the loss of data. I've been a straight A student all my life and now there is no record of that. In school we are always hearing about something going on our permanent record. Turns out it's not so permanent.

On the other hand the banks, car dealers, and credit card companies don't have any records either so they can't repo what they don't know about or can't prove.

It turns out that a lot of the government and financial institutions actually have backup copies of birth certificates, titles, and deeds on <u>microfilm</u> stored somewhere in a cave in Kansas. However it appears that the storage place was ransacked and some of the contents were used for firewood. They are estimating it will take years to restore this data.

Luckily my family had paid the farm off a long time ago and we have this old style deed that was actually recorded on paper and kept in a rather large safe in my parent's closet.

I remember on several occasions in the past mom trying to get dad to buy one of the scanners that you are always seeing advertised on T.V. You know the one that will eliminate piles of paper and clutter and reduce it down to a few simple, easy to find, files on your computer. Some time I'm glad dad is stuck in his old ways.

The president is trying to keep his promise and fix things. He has issued a moratorium on any finical transactions that are not required to sustain life. What that amounts to is no one is allowed to spend money on anything other than food, medicine, or gasoline. No power bills, water bills, car payment, etc. until the infrastructure is back up and running and data is restored.

The power, water, and gas companies have to furnish service to their customers for free until the President says otherwise.

All in All it's been very quiet around here. People are beginning to find out that Molly and I are the ones that the President was talking about in his speech and they come by every now and then to thank me or pump me for information. The sheriff and Donna come by almost daily to check on me. Even Murphy has come by a couple of times to make sure I'm ok. I love having them come by but I wish we had something else to talk about.

Mom and dad have gone off the deep end. They have to know where I'm at every second of the day. You would think that with a humvee full of soldiers still driving around the farm watching over us they would relax a little bit.

With schools being closed I have plenty of time to go horseback riding. Zoe loves the extra attention but Murdock feels left out so Molly comes over to go riding with me. When we are not riding we just hang out and listen to music. We don't talk much. She is going through what most people would call Post-Traumatic Stress Disorder.

During the time that we were going through this ordeal she was a real trooper and never showed any signs of freaking out. Now that it's all over she has become very irritable, introverted, and is constantly looking over her shoulder. Unfortunately I know how she feels.

I hope more than anything that our friendship survives all of this. I love her very much but every time we look at each other we instantly flash back to something we went through. If time doesn't fix this then I'm afraid we will get to a point to where we will avoid each other just to keep from re-living the past. But everyone is really trying to help us get through it. Tom Poulos sent a counselor by to talk to us and she said we need to keep this stuff out in the open and talk about it but it's really hard.

Shane is in sort of a witness protection program. His <u>real</u> grandparents are taking care of the farm but Shane, his mom, and his dad just vanished. It sucks not being able to hang out with him but I understand it is going to take some time for it to be safe for him around here. I really do miss him. Mom lets me ride over to his farm as often as I want to. Of course there is always a Humvee full of soldiers following along behind me. I think mom really understands but I still use the excuse that I want Zoe to get to see Fat Biscuit, and I do, but I just like to go over and hang out so I can be reminded of how much Shane and his friendship really means to me.

About two weeks ago a mysterious box appeared on the front porch. After talking dad out of watering it down with the water hose one of the soldiers opened it to find a new laptop. It was addressed to me but had no return address. It had all my favorite music and software loaded on it along with a bunch of Photoshopped pictures.

Even though there was no return address the wallpaper instantly gave away who it was from. I only know one person that would have used a picture of the Hopes and Dreams statue as wallpaper. I got the message. It's not like I haven't been checking every time we go to town.

So that's pretty much how it happened. No names were changed to protect the innocent or any of that. Just the facts the best I remember them. I hope that history will prove that we did the right thing.

SYNOPSIS

The small, sleepy town of Perry, Oklahoma, is known for being the home of Ditch Witch and the capture of Timothy McVeigh. But one of its residents has played a key role in the technological apocalypse people have come to call the Day of the Monarch.

Despite the lack of electricity from a power outage, Christmas morning starts much like any other for twelve-year-old Abby Tate, but things quickly spiral into chaos. Not only has the power outage affected the state, but according to short-wave radio, it's impacted the entire world.

Abbey's computer-savvy friend, Shane, insists he is the cause of the power outage. His computer virus, the Monarch Virus, destroys a computer's microprocessor and ram chips, and he thinks it is responsible for the world-wide blackout. Abby doesn't believe him—until Shane goes missing and a fleet of military forces takes over the town.

But something doesn't make sense. Does the government have Shane in custody to prevent other countries from using him and his virus as a weapon? When FEMA sets up camp on Abby's family farm, she swings into action, recruiting her friend Molly to begin investigating and having no idea of just how much danger she's about to encounter.

R obert E. Hill's extensive resume covers everything from electro-optical engineer to Baptist preacher. He is the author of several screenplays, including *Forever Nineteen* and *Final Revelation*, as well as the nonfiction book, *Throwaway People*. He currently lives in Nevada.